FAMILY TIES

male / female

natural / social

big / small

animal / human

Works w/ binaries to social critique

speech / silence

life / death

binaries are
assembled
to deconstruct

The Texas Pan American Series

the gaze as
being an
act of
consumption.

CLARICE LISPECTOR

Family Ties

(Laços de Família)

Translated with an Introduction by
GIOVANNI PONTIERO

 UNIVERSITY OF TEXAS PRESS

AUSTIN

Translated from *Laços de Família*
Copyright © 1960 by Clarice Lispector

Library of Congress Cataloging-in-Publication Data

Lispector, Clarice.
  Family ties.

  (Texas pan American series)
  Bibliography: p.
  CONTENTS: The daydreams of a drunk woman.—
Love—The chicken. [etc.]
  I. Title.
PZ4.L769Fam [PQ9697.L585] 869'.3 72-412
ISBN 978-0-292-72448-8 (cloth: alk.paper)

Requests for permission to reproduce material from
this work should be sent to:
  Permissions
  University of Texas Press
  P.O. Box 7819
  Austin, TX 78713-7819

  utpress.utexas.edu/index.php/rp-form

∞The paper used in this book meets the minimum
requirements of ANSI/NISO Z39.48-1992 (R1997)
(Permanence of Paper).

FOR ARNOLD,

with gratitude

WORKS BY CLARICE LISPECTOR

NOVELS

Perto do Coração Selvagem [Close to the savage heart]. Rio: A Noite, 1944. (Awarded the Graça Aranha Prize)

O Lustre [The Chandelier]. Rio: Agir, 1946.

A Cidade Sitiada [The besieged city]. Rio: A Noite, 1948.

A Maçã no Escuro [The apple in the dark]. Rio: Livraria F. Alves, 1961.

A Paixão Segundo G. H. [The passion according to G. H.]. Rio: Editôra do Autor, 1964.

Uma Aprendizagem ou o Livro dos Prazeres [An apprenticeship or the book of delights]. Rio: Editôra Sabiá, 1969.

SHORT STORIES

Alguns Contos [Some stories]. Rio: Ministério de Educação, 1952.

Laços de Família [Family ties]. Rio: Editôra do Autor, 1960. (Awarded the Jabuti Prize)

A Legião Estrangeira [The foreign legion]. Rio: Editôra do Autor, 1964.

Felicidade Clandestina [Secret happiness]. Rio: Editôra Sabiá, 1971.

BOOKS FOR CHILDREN

O Mistério do Coelho Pensante [The mystery of the thoughtful rabbit]. Rio: José Alvaro, 1967.

A Mulher que Matou os Peixes [The woman who killed the fishes]. Rio: Editôra Sabiá, 1968.

CONTENTS

ACKNOWLEDGMENTS

I wish to express my deep gratitude to Sr. Eudinyr Fraga, who first introduced me to these stories by Clarice Lispector, and to the author herself, who encouraged me to attempt an English translation; to Dr. A. P. Hinchliffe who patiently read, reread, and cogently revised the manuscript; to Mr. Norman Lamb, Dr. R. C. Willis, and Mrs. Maria Teresa Rogers, who offered much valuable advice and criticism; and also to Miss Jennifer Orford, Mrs. Nancy Stålhammer, and Miss Mary MacDonald, who typed the manuscript with infinite care.

Acknowledgment is also due to the director of the Hispanic and Luso-Brazilian Councils at Canning House for permission to reproduce the translation of "Amor," which was originally submitted for the Camoens Awards, 1968. And finally a special note of thanks to Professor Fred P. Ellison of the University of Texas at Austin for his painstaking corrections to the manuscript in its various stages of preparation and his unfailing encouragement in the face of inevitable problems.

G.P.

INTRODUCTION

Clarice Lispector was born in Tchetchelnik, Ukraine, on December 10, 1925. Her parents were Russian, but the family emigrated to Brazil when she was only two months old, and she spent her childhood at Recife in the northeastern state of Pernambuco. Here she began her education before moving at the age of twelve to Rio where she continued her studies. A precocious interest in literature led her to write short stories and plays while still in her teens. Her own revelations about her subsequent literary formation indicate a somewhat ambitious and comprehensive absorption of contemporary Brazilian writing alongside a consistently widening range of foreign works, which notably include a special interest in the narratives of Katherine Mansfield, Virginia Woolf, and Rosamund Lehmann. While still an undergraduate at the National Faculty of Law, Clarice Lispector began to gain experience in journalism, first on the editorial staff of the Agência Nacional, and then with A Noite. 1944 was a particularly eventful year for her; shortly after graduation she married a fellow student, and in the same year she published her first novel, *Perto do Coração Selvagem* [Close to the savage heart].

Her husband's career as a diplomat gave Clarice Lispector the opportunity to travel and spend long periods living abroad. From 1945 to 1949 the couple lived in Europe and from 1952 until 1960 in the United States.

From the outset her potential as a novelist was recognized by reviewers. Brazilian critics expressed a wholehearted admiration for the extraordinary insights and rare intensity of expression she showed in this first novel. Since then, a steady output of novels and collections of short stories has confirmed their hopes that Brazil had found a young writer of individual talent and originality working in the mainstream of existentialist writing; her reputation has been firmly established with works like *Laços de Família* [Family ties] and *A Paixão Segundo G. H.* [The passion according to G. H.]. It is generally agreed among her critics, however, that her true medium lies in the shorter forms of fiction, and the stories of *Laços de Família* give a comprehensive picture of the author's private world of deep psychological complexities. The narrative in these stories often appears to evolve from smoke—from some momentary experience or minor episode that seems quite insignificant in itself. Action, as such, is virtually nonexistent, and the threads of tension are maintained by use of stream-of-consciousness techniques and interior monologues frequently sustained by a single character. This creates an intensely personal note in Clarice Lispector's writing that can often give the impression of being labored and excessive in some of her novels, yet is unfailingly effective in her stories, where the brilliant flashes of insight are less exposed to repetition. In her stories commonplace situations and dream fantasies meet and merge, the most poetic prose mingling with realistic observation. Obvious examples are "The Imitation of the Rose," "Preciousness," and, above all, "Mystery in São Cristóvão," where, without exactly losing contact with the real world, the reader is invited to explore the nebulous domains of the subconscious. As Wilson Martins rightly observed in a review of "The Imitation of the Rose," the rarefied atmosphere and subtlety of this story, which hovers on the extreme confines of the spirit, on those uncertain boundaries between health and insanity, between light and darkness, found its only possible author in Clarice Lispector.

Influenced by existentialist writers, Clarice Lispector shows an almost obsessive preoccupation with the themes of human suffering and failure, the disconcerting implications of our humanity, the hunger of the solitary man hemmed in by hostile forces, his awareness of inevitable alienation and the pressing need to overcome its dangers, and most forcefully of all, his terror upon recognizing the ultimate nothingness. In a scrupulous analysis of the philosophical thought implicit in her writing, the Brazilian critic Benedito Nunes finds echoes of Kierkegaard and Heidegger and their grim vision of human existence, but most convincingly of all the writer's close parallels with the fundamental theories of Camus and Sartre. Her debt to Sartre's theory of existentialism is clear. Like the French writer, Clarice Lispector emphasizes the opposition between sincerity and bad faith, although her conclusions are invariably more pessimistic. Bad faith, according to Sartre, consists in pretending to ourselves and others that things could not be otherwise—that we are bound to our way of life, and that we could not escape it even if we wanted to. Most appeals, therefore, to duty or deeply rooted creeds are to be seen as instances of bad faith, since we are free to choose to do all these things and we need not do them.

A similar dilemma provokes the violent emotional crises that haunt and defeat the characters in these stories. Human freedom, which brings anguish, springs from man's recognition of nothingness. Anguish comes when man becomes aware of the gulf between himself and his possibilities. He must inevitably choose between them, and whatever he chooses makes him what he is. Like the "sincere" man described by Sartre in his first novel, *La Nausée* (*Nausea*), Lispector's characters, too, face nothingness and experience nausea. Like Roquentin, her characters come to realize that nausea is a part of themselves, indeed integral to their very nature in relation to other things and other people.

Clarice Lispector explores that tortured ambiguity of our existence; the privilege and the curse of being human and of confronting both our absolute freedom and the world's indifference—in short, the condition Camus describes as Absurdity. Her treatment of this vital condition coincides fully with the definition and examples of Absurdity offered by Camus in *Le Mythe de Sisyphe* (*The Myth of Sisyphus*).

Her characters experience that feeling of Absurdity Camus has described, that certain *mal*, sickness, or evil prevalent in the sensibility of contemporary society, which can strike any man in the face on any street corner. The stories of *Laços de Família* explore the four possible ways defined by Camus in order to arrive at this sudden birth of feeling:

1. The mechanical nature of many peoples lives may lead them to question the value and purpose of their existence, and this is an intimation of Absurdity (e.g., Anna in "Love" and the old woman in "Happy Birthday").

2. An acute sense of time passing, or the recognition that time is a destructive force (e.g., "The Chicken" and "The Imitation of the Rose")—an experience linked with a haunting awareness of certain death.

3. The sense of being in an alien world. Alienation to the point of nausea when confronted with the arbitrary nature of our existence—when familiar objects normally "domesticated" by names, such as flower, dog, bus, stone, tree, are unexpectedly robbed of their familiarity (e.g., "The Crime of the Mathematics Professor" and "The Beginnings of a Fortune").

4. A sense of inexorable isolation from other beings—forcibly present in nearly all of these stories and predominantly so in "Preciousness" and "The Buffalo."

The lesson of these experiences, in brief, is that human life is Absurd in that there can be no final justification for our projects. Everyone is *de trop*. Everything is dispensable—a situation played out with an element of tragic comedy in "The Smallest Woman in the World," where the readers of a color supplement feel anguish and nausea at recognizing the Absurdity of an unexpected discovery in the jungle. How ought they to behave? To what extent are they free?

Probing the way in which consciousness perceives objects, Lispector creates a world of exciting and terrifying perceptions. Nunes has defined the process as "uma espécie de mergulho nas potências obscuras da vida"—familiar situations and things which we think we know and can control, are suddenly transformed into something strange, unexpected, and uncontrollable. Moods are carefully varied between the disquieting tension of silence to a frenzy of passion—a climax illustrated by the old woman spitting aggressively on the floor in "Happy Birthday" or the final swoon in "The Buffalo."

Mysterious and quite unexpected moments of crisis propel characters along the paths of indecision to a crucial moment of self-discovery. At times the most trivial episode can produce the most profound and dramatic intuition—the vital moment when time stands still and our daily existence is stripped bare of its comfortable conventional surfaces, leaving man alone in the solitude of his conscience and his personality. Man's real problem, however, is not that of imposing some meaning on his senseless existence, but of finding some escape from the meaning he has already discovered within himself and refuses to accept.

The men and women Lispector describes are driven to the extreme limits of their potential and show in their anguish both their greatness and their misery; they are great because of this suddenly discovered freedom and yet miserable because they are capable of every kind of weakness when faced with such an absolute responsibility. Such is the plight of Anna, who disintegrates spiritually after her encounter with the blind love in "Love"; of Laura in "The Imitation of the Rose," who is recovering from a nervous breakdown; and of the disturbed onlooker in the restaurant in "The Dinner." This paradox in human existence also helps to explain the complex emotions in "The Daydreams of a Drunk Woman" and "The Crime of the Mathematics Professor" with its theme of expiation.

Alarmed at the dangers of existing, the protagonists of these stories face crises that hover between fantasy and realism, crises they cannot fully understand. In "Love" we are reminded of Kafka's vision of the world, which is full of signs we are unable to understand, but in "The Buffalo" we are back with Camus, who sees the human predicament stemming from the absence of any such signs.

Suddenly conscious of an absolute freedom, her characters find themselves unable either to ignore or to transcend this condition. They hang between a tangible recognizable reality and an obscure sense of the mysterious; they witness, without being able to react, the metamorphosis of places and people, as emotion transforms the world. The idyllic peace of the botanical gardens in "Love" becomes a place of strange agitated forces—a place disturbed by the sudden absence of law and order clearly reminiscent of the haunted park of Bouville described by Sartre in *La Nausée*. Clarice Lispector also exploits the existentialist image of the universe seen as a great machine capable of creating life and death. Nature is seen as the pure fact of being, the state of being-in-itself. At times it is represented as a mass of sickening objects, viscous, cloying, and showing a richness bordering on putrefaction; that nausea, produced by disquieting associations of color and substance (e.g., spoiled meat or fresh blood) and that disgust when we apprehend what Sarte has called the "viscosity" of things in *L'Etre et le néant* (*Being and Nothingness*).

The characters created by Clarice Lispector defy any obvious or straightforward classification. They cannot, for example, be described as "types" even in a psychological context. Indeed, it might be more appropriate to see them as images of different states of mind. And this applies also to her settings: the gardens and parks in "Love" and "The Buffalo," the urban scenes in "Preciousness" and "The Daydreams of a Drunk Woman," and the jungle setting of "The Smallest Woman in the World" all exist outside time and space. People and settings in these stories, however particular, personal, and subjective, ultimately reflect a profounder reality that is both impersonal and transcendental. From this we can see that Clarice Lispector is a writer who is not interested primarily in the individuals and their private contexts but in the passions that dominate and usually defeat them. There is, nevertheless, nothing spectral or phantasmagorical about her men and women, or her landscapes. Moved by their desire to exist, this very desire becomes the source of their worldly ambitions. Hence the bitterness of their failures and the inseparable relationship between human anguish and the dilemma of existence. Like Sartre and Camus, Clarice Lispector subscribes to the idea that acts alone are important— and isolation and violence become the two salient features of human experience.

Encounters with the animal world are frequent in her stories. The animals of Clarice Lispector are drawn with exceptional vigor and precision, and define the vital links with primitive life. Her animals, symbolizing brute existence, embody all that is obvious and sentient in a reality that is primordial—a reality intensified in these stories. Thus the chicken, the dog, and the buffalo, because they are unable to form judgments about their existence, are able to experience the "pure emotions" of love and hatred, of pain and pleasure. Untouched by human contradictions, animals are more alive because they are more secure than human beings. Free from psychological conflicts, they show a greater participation of what is real—of the greater space that includes all spaces.

The strength and compelling nature of Clarice Lispector's writing bring her to the very heart of the varied and complex experiences she deals with. Stories like "The Daydreams of a Drunk Woman," "Love," and "Family Ties" create a special world of feminine intuition and fancy. Here the author cautiously probes the vulnerability and compassion of her sex. The troubled period of adolescence is treated delicately and with an extraordinary degree of tact and understanding in "Preciousness" and "The Beginnings of a Fortune," while "The Imitation of the Rose," with its poignant account of a woman's faltering attempt to return to domestic harmony after a nervous illness only to end in a relapse when betrayed by her love of beauty and perfection, is very much a tour de force. In exploring the tenuous links of the most intimate human relationships, Clarice Lispector brings us to a heightened awareness of our human condition: the narrow divide between success and failure, the mental and physical stratagems by which we struggle toward a compromise with reality, trying in vain to disguise our vulnerable state. The ironies and innuendoes of "Happy Birthday" and "The Smallest Woman in the World" reveal what they seek to conceal, the fears and apprehensions of human nature, the interior voices which must be silenced, the pettiness of betrayals, the meanness of our little hypocrisies, and the truths we dare not confide, even to ourselves, and the silent arguments we erect in our efforts to justify our passions and desires.

Human motives are revealed with a terrible frankness: our insatiable hunger to possess and to be possessed, the dark disorders behind the masks convention obliges us to wear, the bitter sense of alienation experienced even when we are with those bound to us by blood and kinship, the fears and doubts which daily consume us in the trap of existence, and the supreme moments of crisis which we are condemned to face alone. Hence the ambiguity of the word *laços* (ties)—referring on the one hand to the social chains of conformity which link each human to his fellow man, on the other hand to the bonds of solitude and alienation inherent in our humanity.

Sometimes the narration seems touched by magic, and the dream sequences, as in "Mystery in São Cristóvão," emphasize both the terror and beauty in life—the poetry of that spirit which is truly ineffable when concerned with self-discovery and adventure. Elsewhere, Clarice Lispector uses fiercer passions, as in "The Buffalo" where a woman who has been abandoned by her lover goes to the zoological gardens to find there creatures who represent her hate and self-destruction; or in "The Crime of the Mathematics Professor" with its relentless voices of guilt—the cruel exposure of the rituals we play out in private—or the uncomfortable sensations of brutal indifference and destruction in "The Dinner."

The writer's complex and probing attitude to man's existence raises fundamental philosophical questions, which she chooses to express in rich metaphors often borrowed from the world of classical myth and ritual in order to describe the solemnity and magnitude of human experience. In her prose style, Clarice Lispector has come close to achieving that "fertility and fluency" of expression avidly described by Virginia Woolf in *A Writer's Diary* (London, 1953). Like the English novelist, she also appears to be learning her craft in the most fierce conditions—one moment confronted by the brutality and wildness of the world, "l'hostilité primitive du monde" (to quote Camus), the next moment overcome by the poetry of life. In this "dialogue of the soul with the soul," Clarice Lispector, too, is intent upon capturing the inexpressible in her narrative by means of unorthodox syntactical structures, staccato rhythms, and the obsessive repetition of certain key words and symbols—aptly described by Nunes as "um efeito mágico de refluxo da linguagem que deixa à

mostra o *aquilo*, o inexpressado." The conflict between an interior and external world, between existence and thought, is thus
extended to a conflict between existence and the linguistic expression of existence. Nausea, as Sartre has already shown,
exists on more than one level and leads us to examine an old
and familiar metaphysical doubt—the relation of words to the
thing described. Clarice Lispector shares the Sartrean convic-
tion that we are not content to live. We need to know who we
are, to understand our nature, and to express it. Her vision of
reality gives identity to being and nothingness and satisfies the
need "to speak of that which obliges us to be silent."

The following studies have been closely consulted for this
essay and are especially recommended for further reading:

Clarice Lispector

Benedito Nunes, *O Mundo de Clarice Lispector* (Manaus:
Edições do Governo do Estado, 1966) and "O Mundo Imagi-
nário de Clarice Lispector," in *O Dorso do Tigre* (São Paulo:
Editôra Perspectiva, 1969). Rita Herman, "Existence in *Laços
de Família*," *Luso-Brazilian Review* 4, no. 1 (June 1967), Uni-
versity of Wisconsin Press. Massaud Moisés, *Temas Brasileiros*
(São Paulo: Conselho Estadual de Cultura, 1964). Renard
Perez, *Escritores Brasileiros*, 2nd series, Editôra Civilização
Brasileira, 1964. Two essays in *Studies in Short Fiction* 7, no. 1
(Winter 1971), Newberry College, South Carolina: Giovanni
Pontiero, "The Drama of Existence in *Laços de Família*," pp.
256–267, and Massaud Moisés, "Clarice Lispector: Fiction and
Cosmic Vision," pp. 268–281.

Jean-Paul Sartre

Iris Murdoch, *Sartre, Romantic Rationalist: Studies in Modern
European Literature and Thought* (London: Bowes, 1961).
The Philosophy of Jean-Paul Sartre, edited by Robert Denoon

Cumming (New York: Random House, 1965). Anthony Manser, *Sartre: A Philosophic Study* (London: Athlone Press, 1966). Mary Warnock, *The Philosophy of Sartre* (London: Hutchinson, 1966). Jean-Paul Sartre, *Nausea*, translated by Robert Baldick (London: Penguin, 1965).

Albert Camus

John Cruikshank, *Albert Camus and the Literature of Revolt* (London: Oxford University Press, 1959). Germaine Brée, *Camus* (New Brunswick, N.J.: Rutgers University Press, 1959). Philip Thody, *Albert Camus 1913–1960* (London: Hamish Hamilton, 1961). Albert Camus, *Lyrical and Critical Essays*, selected and translated from the French by Philip Thody (London: Hamish Hamilton, 1967).

FAMILY TIES

The Daydreams of a Drunk Woman

It seemed to her that the trolley cars were about to cross through the room as they caused her reflected image to tremble. She was combing her hair at her leisure in front of the dressing table with its three mirrors, and her strong white arms shivered in the coolness of the evening. Her eyes did not look away as the mirrors trembled, sometimes dark, sometimes luminous. Outside, from a window above, something heavy and hollow fell to the ground. Had her husband and the little ones been at home, the idea would already have occurred to her that they were to blame. Her eyes did not take themselves off her image, her comb worked pensively, and her open dressing gown revealed in the mirrors the intersected breasts of several women.

"Evening News" shouted the newsboy to the mild breeze in Riachuelo Street, and something trembled as if foretold. She threw her comb down on the dressing table and sang dreamily: "Who saw the little spar-row . . . it passed by the window . . . and flew beyond Minho!"—but, suddenly becoming irritated, she shut up abruptly like a fan.

She lay down and fanned herself impatiently with a newspaper that rustled in the room. She clutched the bedsheet, inhaling its odor as she crushed its starched embroidery with her red-lacquered nails. Then, almost smiling, she started to fan herself once more. Oh my!—she sighed as she began to smile. She beheld the picture of her bright smile, the smile of a woman who was still young, and she continued to smile to herself, closing her eyes and fanning herself still more vigorously. Oh my!—she would come fluttering in from the street like a butterfly.

"Hey there! Guess who came to see me today?" she mused as a feasible and interesting topic of conversation. "No idea, tell me," those eyes asked her with a gallant smile, those sad eyes set in one of those pale faces that make one feel so uncomfortable. "Maria Quiteria, my dear!" she replied coquettishly with her hand on her hip. "And who, might we ask, would she be?" they insisted gallantly, but now without any expression. "You!" she broke off, slightly annoyed. How boring!

Oh what a succulent room! Here she was, fanning herself in Brazil. The sun, trapped in the blinds, shimmered on the wall like the strings of a guitar. Riachuelo Street shook under the gasping weight of the trolley cars which came from Mem de Sá Street. Curious and impatient, she listened to the vibrations of the china cabinet in the drawing room. Impatiently she rolled over to lie face downward, and, sensuously stretching the toes of her dainty feet, she awaited her next thought with open eyes. "Whosoever found, searched," she said to herself in the form of a rhymed refrain, which always ended up by sounding like some maxim. Until eventually she fell asleep with her mouth wide open, her saliva staining the pillow.

She only woke up when her husband came into the room the moment he returned from work. She did not want to eat any dinner nor to abandon her dreams, and she went back to sleep: let him content himself with the leftovers from lunch.

And now that the kids were at the country house of their aunts in Jacarepaguá, she took advantage of their absence in order to begin the day as she pleased: restless and frivolous in her bed . . . one of those whims perhaps. Her husband appeared before her, having already dressed, and she did not even know what he had prepared for his breakfast. She avoided examining his suit to see whether it needed brushing . . . little did she care if this was his day for attending to his business in the city. But when he bent over to kiss her, her capriciousness crackled like a dry leaf.

"Don't paw me!"

"What the devil's the matter with you?" the man asked her in amazement, as he immediately set about attempting some more effective caress.

Obstinate, she would not have known what to reply, and she felt so touchy and aloof that she did not even know where to find a suitable reply. She suddenly lost her temper. "Go to hell! . . . prowling round me like some old tomcat."

He seemed to think more clearly and said, firmly, "You're ill, my girl."

She accepted his remark, surprised, and vaguely flattered.

She remained in bed the whole day long listening to the silence of the house without the scurrying of the kids, without her husband who would have his meals in the city today. Her anger was tenuous and ardent. She only got up to go to the bathroom, from which she returned haughty and offended.

The morning turned into a long enormous afternoon, which then turned into a shallow night, which innocently dawned throughout the entire house.

She was still in bed, peaceful and casual. She was in love. . . . She was anticipating her love for the man whom she would love one day. Who knows, this sometimes happened, and without any guilt or injury for either partner. Lying in bed thinking and thinking, and almost laughing as one does over some gossip. Thinking and thinking. About what? As if she knew. So she just stayed there.

The next minute she would get up, angry. But in the weakness of that first instant she felt dizzy and fragile in the room which swam round and round until she managed to grope her way back to bed, amazed that it might be true. "Hey, girl, don't you go getting sick on me!" she muttered suspiciously. She raised her hand to her forehead to see if there was any fever.

That night, until she fell asleep, her mind became more and more delirious—for how many minutes?—until she flopped over, fast asleep, to snore beside her husband.

She awoke late, the potatoes waiting to be peeled, the kids expected home that same evening from their visit to the country. "God, I've lost my self-respect, I have! My day for washing and darning socks. . . . What a lazy bitch you've turned out to be!" she scolded herself, inquisitive and pleased . . . shopping to be done, fish to remember, already so late on a hectic sunny morning.

But on Saturday night they went to the tavern in Tiradentes Square at the invitation of a rich businessman, she with her new dress which didn't have any fancy trimmings but was made of good material, a dress that would last her a lifetime. On Saturday night, drunk in Tiradentes Square, inebriated but with her husband at her side to give her support, and being very polite in front of the other man who was so much more refined and rich—striving to make conversation, for she was no provincial ninny and she had already experienced life in the capital. But so drunk that she could no longer stand.

And if her husband was not drunk it was only because he did not want to show disrespect for the businessman, and, full of solicitude and humility, he left the swaggering to the other fellow. His manner suited such an elegant occasion, but it gave her such an urge to laugh! She despised him beyond words! She looked at her husband stuffed into his new suit and found him so ridiculous! . . . so drunk that she could no longer stand, but without losing her self-respect as a woman. And the green wine from her native Portugal slowly being drained from her glass.

When she got drunk, as if she had eaten a heavy Sunday lunch, all things which by their true nature are separate from each other—the smell of oil on the one hand, of a male on the other; the soup tureen on the one hand, the waiter on the other —became strangely linked by their true nature and the whole thing was nothing short of disgraceful . . . shocking!

And if her eyes appeared brilliant and cold, if her movements faltered clumsily until she succeeded in reaching the toothpick holder, beneath the surface she really felt so far quite at ease . . . there was that full cloud to transport her without effort. Her puffy lips, her teeth white, and her body swollen with wine. And the vanity of feeling drunk, making her show such disdain for everything, making her feel swollen and rotund like a large cow.

Naturally she talked, since she lacked neither the ability to converse nor topics to discuss. But the words that a woman uttered when drunk were like being pregnant—mere words on her lips which had nothing to do with the secret core that seemed like a pregnancy. God, how queer she felt! Saturday night, her every-day soul lost, and how satisfying to lose it, and to remind her of former days, only her small, ill-kempt hands— and here she was now with her elbows resting on the white and red checked tablecloth like a gambling table, deeply launched upon a degrading and revolting existence. And what about her laughter? . . . this outburst of laughter which mysteriously emerged from her full white throat, in response to the polite manners of the businessman, an outburst of laughter coming from the depths of that sleep, and from the depths of that security of someone who has a body. Her white flesh was as sweet as lobster, the legs of a live lobster wriggling slowly in the air . . . that urge to be sick in order to plunge that sweetness into something really awful . . . and that perversity of someone who has a body.

She talked and listened with curiosity to what she herself was about to reply to the well-to-do businessman who had so kindly invited them out to dinner and paid for their meal. Intrigued and amazed, she heard what she was on the point of replying, and what she might say in her present state would serve as an augury for the future. She was no longer a lobster, but a harsher sign—that of the scorpion. After all, she had been born in November.

A beacon that sweeps through the dawn while one is asleep, such was her drunkenness which floated slowly through the air.

At the same time, she was conscious of such feelings! Such feelings! When she gazed upon that picture which was so beautifully painted in the restaurant, she was immediately overcome by an artistic sensibility. No one would get it out of her head that she had really been born for greater things. She had always been one for works of art.

But such sensibility! And not merely excited by the picture of grapes and pears and dead fish with shining scales. Her sensibility irritated her without causing her pain, like a broken fingernail. And if she wanted, she could allow herself the luxury of becoming even more sensitive, she could go still further, because she was protected by a situation, protected like everyone who had attained a position in life. Like someone saved from misfortune. I'm so miserable, dear God! If she wished, she could even pour more wine into her glass, and, protected by the position which she had attained in life, become even more drunk just so long as she did not lose her self-respect. And so, even more drunk, she peered round the room, and how she despised the barren people in that restaurant. Not a real man among them. How sad it really all seemed. How she despised the barren people in that restaurant, while she was plump and heavy and generous to the full. And everything in the restaurant seemed so remote, the one thing distant from the other, as if the one might never be able to converse with the other. Each existing for itself, and God existing there for everyone.

Her eyes once more settled on that female whom she had instantly detested the moment she had entered the room. Upon arriving, she had spotted her seated at a table accompanied by a man and all dolled up in a hat and jewelry, glittering like a false coin, all coy and refined. What a fine hat she was wearing! . . . Bet you anything she isn't even married for all that pious look on her face . . . and that fine hat stuck on her head. A fat lot of good her hypocrisy would do her, and she had better watch out in case her airs and graces proved her undoing! The more sanctimonious they were, the bigger frauds they turned out to be. And as for the waiter, he was a great nitwit, serving her, full of gestures and finesse, while the sallow man with her pretended not to notice. And that pious ninny so pleased with herself in that hat and so modest about her slim waistline, and I'll bet she couldn't even bear her man a child. All right, it was none of her business, but from the moment she arrived she felt the urge to give that blonde prude of a woman playing the grand lady in her hat a few good slaps on the face. She didn't even have any shape, and she was flat-chested. And no doubt, for all her fine hats, she was nothing more than a fishwife trying to pass herself off as a duchess.

Oh, how humiliated she felt at having come to the bar without a hat, and her head now felt bare. And that madam with her affectations, playing the refined lady! I know what you need, my beauty, you and your sallow boy friend! And if you think I envy you with your flat chest, let me assure you that I don't give a damn for you and your hats. Shameless sluts like you are only asking for a good hard slap on the face.

In her holy rage, she stretched out a shaky hand and reached for a toothpick.

But finally, the difficulty of arriving home disappeared; she now bestirred herself amidst the familiar reality of her room, now seated on the edge of the bed, a slipper dangling from one foot.

And, as she had half closed her blurred eyes, everything took on the appearance of flesh, the foot of the bed, the window, the suit her husband had thrown off, and everything became rather painful. Meanwhile, she was becoming larger, more unsteady, swollen and gigantic. If only she could get closer to herself, she would find she was even larger. Each of her arms could be explored by someone who didn't even recognize that they were dealing with an arm, and someone could plunge into each eye and swim around without knowing that it was an eye. And all around her everything was a bit painful. Things of the flesh stricken by nervous twinges. The chilly air had caught her as she had come out of the restaurant.

She was sitting up in bed, resigned and sceptical. And this was nothing yet, God only knew—she was perfectly aware that this was nothing yet. At this moment things were happening to her that would only hurt later and in earnest. When restored to her normal size, her anesthetized body would start to wake up, throbbing, and she would begin to pay for those big meals and drinks. Then, since this would really end up by happening, I might as well open my eyes right now (which she did) and then everything looked smaller and clearer, without her feeling any pain. Everything, deep down, was the same, only smaller and more familiar. She was sitting quite upright in bed, her stomach so full, absorbed and resigned, with the delicacy of one who sits waiting until her partner awakens. "You gorge yourself and I pay the piper," she said sadly, looking at the dainty white toes of her feet. She looked around her, patient and obedient. Ah, words, nothing but words, the objects in the room lined up in the order of words, to form those confused and irksome phrases that he who knows how will read. Boredom . . . such awful boredom. . . . How sickening! How very annoying! When all is said and done, heaven help me—God knows best. What was one to do? How can I describe this thing inside me? Anyhow, God knows best. And to think that she had enjoyed herself so much last night! . . . and to think of how nice it all was—a restaurant to her liking—and how she had been seated elegantly at table. At table! The world would exclaim. But she made no reply, drawing herself erect with a bad-tempered click of her tongue . . . irritated . . . "Don't come to me with your endearments" . . . disenchanted, resigned, satiated, married, content, vaguely nauseated.

It was at this moment that she became deaf: one of her senses was missing. She clapped the palm of her hand over her ear, which only made things worse . . . suddenly filling her eardrum with the whirr of an elevator . . . life suddenly becoming loud and magnified in its smallest movements. One of two things: either she was deaf or hearing all too well. She reacted against this new suggestion with a sensation of spite and annoyance, with a sigh of resigned satiety. "Drop dead," she said gently . . . defeated.

"And when in the restaurant . . ." she suddenly recalled when she had been in the restaurant her husband's protector had pressed his foot against hers beneath the table, and above the table his face was watching her. By coincidence or intentionally? The rascal. A fellow, to be frank, who was not unattractive. She shrugged her shoulders.

And when above the roundness of her low-cut dress—right in the middle of Tiradentes Square! she thought, shaking her head incredulously—that fly had settled on her bare bosom. What cheek!

Certain things were good because they were almost nauseating . . . the noise like that of an elevator in her blood, while her husband lay snoring at her side . . . her chubby little children sleeping in the other room, the little villains. Ah, what's wrong with me! she wondered desperately. Have I eaten too much? Heavens above! What *is* wrong with me?

It was unhappiness.

Her toes playing with her slipper . . . the floor not too clean at that spot. "What a slovenly, lazy bitch you've become."

Not tomorrow, because her legs would not be too steady, but the day after tomorrow that house of hers would be a sight worth seeing: she would give it a scouring with soap and water which would get rid of all the dirt! "You mark my words," she threatened in her rage. Ah, she was feeling so well, so strong, as if she still had milk in those firm breasts. When her husband's friend saw her so pretty and plump he had immediately felt respect for her. And when she started to get embarrassed she did not know which way to look. Such misery! What was one to do? Seated on the edge of the bed, blinking in resignation. How well one could see the moon on these summer nights. She leaned over slightly, indifferent and resigned. The moon! How clearly one could see it. The moon high and yellow gliding through the sky, poor thing. Gliding, gliding . . . high up, high up. The moon! Then her vulgarity exploded in a sudden outburst of affection; "you slut", she cried out, laughing.

Love

Feeling a little tired, with her purchases bulging her new string bag, Anna boarded the tram. She placed the bag on her lap and the tram started off. Settling back in her seat she tried to find a comfortable position, with a sigh of mild satisfaction.

Anna had nice children, she reflected with certainty and pleasure. They were growing up, bathing themselves and misbehaving; they were demanding more and more of her time. The kitchen, after all, was spacious with its old stove that made explosive noises. The heat was oppressive in the apartment, which they were paying off in installments, and the wind, playing against the curtains she had made herself, reminded her that if she wanted to she could pause to wipe her forehead, and contemplate the calm horizon. Like a farmer. She had planted the seeds she held in her hand, no others, but only those. And they were growing into trees. Her brisk conversations with the electricity man were growing, the water filling the tank was growing, her children were growing, the table was growing with food, her husband arriving with the newspapers and smiling with hunger, the irritating singing of the maids resounding through the block. Anna tranquilly put her small, strong hand, her life current to everything. Certain times of the afternoon struck her as being critical. At a certain hour of the afternoon the trees she had planted laughed at her. And when nothing more required her strength, she became anxious. Meanwhile she felt herself more solid than ever, her body become a little thicker, and it was worth seeing the manner in which she cut out blouses for the children, the large scissors snapping into the material. All her vaguely artistic aspirations had for some time been channeled into making her days fulfilled and beautiful; with time, her taste for the decorative had developed and supplanted intimate disorder. She seemed to have discovered that everything was capable of being perfected, that each thing could be given a harmonious appearance; life itself could be created by Man.

Deep down, Anna had always found it necessary to feel the firm roots of things. And this is what a home had surprisingly provided. Through tortuous paths, she had achieved a woman's destiny, with the surprise of conforming to it almost as if she had invented that destiny herself. The man whom she had married was a real man, the children she mothered were real children. Her previous youth now seemed alien to her, like one of life's illnesses. She had gradually emerged to discover that life could be lived without happiness: by abolishing it she had found a legion of persons, previously invisible, who lived as one works—with perseverance, persistence, and contentment.

What had happened to Anna before possessing a home of her own stood forever beyond her reach: that disturbing exaltation she had often confused with unbearable happiness. In exchange she had created something ultimately comprehensible, the life of an adult. This was what she had wanted and chosen.

Her precautions were now reduced to alertness during the dangerous part of the afternoon, when the house was empty and she was no longer needed; when the sun reached its zenith, and each member of the family went about his separate duties. Looking at the polished furniture, she felt her heart contract a little with fear. But in her life there was no opportunity to cherish her fears—she suppressed them with that same ingenuity she had acquired from domestic struggles. Then she would go out shopping or take things to be mended, unobtrusively looking after her home and her family. When she returned it would already be late afternoon and the children back from school would absorb her attention. Until the evening descended with its quiet excitement. In the morning she would awaken surrounded by her calm domestic duties. She would find the furniture dusty and dirty once more, as if it had returned repentant. As for herself, she mysteriously formed part of the soft, dark roots of the earth. And anonymously she nourished life. It was pleasant like this. This was what she had wanted and chosen.

The tram swayed on its rails and turned into the main road. Suddenly the wind became more humid, announcing not only the passing of the afternoon but the end of that uncertain hour. Anna sighed with relief and a deep sense of acceptance gave her face an air of womanhood.

The tram would drag along and then suddenly jolt to a halt. As far as Humaitá she could relax. Suddenly she saw the man stationary at the tram stop. The difference between him and others was that he was really stationary. He stood with his hands held out in front of him—blind.

But what else was there about him that made Anna sit up in distrust? Something disquieting was happening. Then she discovered what it was: the blind man was chewing gum . . . a blind man chewing gum. Anna still had time to reflect for a second that her brothers were coming to dinner—her heart pounding at regular intervals. Leaning forward, she studied the blind man intently, as one observes something incapable of returning our gaze. Relaxed, and with open eyes, he was chewing gum in the failing light. The facial movements of his chewing made him appear to smile then suddenly stop smiling, to smile and stop smiling. Anna stared at him as if he had insulted her. And anyone watching would have received the impression of a woman filled with hatred. She continued to stare at him, leaning more and more forward—until the tram gave a sudden jerk, throwing her unexpectedly backward. The heavy string bag toppled from her lap and landed on the floor. Anna cried out, the conductor gave the signal to stop before realizing what was happening, and the tram came to an abrupt halt. The other passengers looked on in amazement. Too paralyzed to gather up her shopping, Anna sat upright, her face suddenly pale. An expression, long since forgotten, awkwardly reappeared, unexpected and inexplicable. The Negro newsboy smiled as he handed over her bundle. The eggs had broken in their newspaper wrapping. Yellow sticky yolks dripped between the strands of the bag. The blind man had interrupted his chewing and held out his unsteady hands, trying in vain to grasp what had happened. She removed the parcel of eggs from the string bag accompanied by the smiles of the passengers. A second signal from the conductor and the tram moved off with another jerk.

A few moments later people were no longer staring at her. The tram was rattling on the rails and the blind man chewing gum had remained behind forever. But the damage had been done.

The string bag felt rough between her fingers, not soft and familiar as when she had knitted it. The bag had lost its meaning; to find herself on that tram was a broken thread; she did not know what to do with the purchases on her lap. Like some strange music, the world started up again around her. The damage had been done. But why? Had she forgotten that there were blind people? Compassion choked her. Anna's breathing became heavy. Even those things which had existed before the episode were now on the alert, more hostile, and even perishable. The world had once more become a nightmare. Several years fell away, the yellow yolks trickled. Exiled from her own days, it seemed to her that the people in the streets were vulnerable, that they barely maintained their equilibrium on the surface of the darkness—and for a moment they appeared to lack any sense of direction. The perception of an absence of law came so unexpectedly that Anna clutched the seat in front of her, as if she might fall off the tram, as if things might be overturned with the same calm they had possessed when order reigned.

What she called a crisis had come at last. And its sign was the intense pleasure with which she now looked at things, suffering and alarmed. The heat had become more oppressive, everything had gained new power and a stronger voice. In the Rua Voluntários da Pátria, revolution seemed imminent, the grids of the gutters were dry, the air dusty. A blind man chewing gum had plunged the world into a mysterious excitement. In every strong person there was a lack of compassion for the blind man, and their strength terrified her. Beside her sat a woman in blue with an expression which made Anna avert her gaze rapidly. On the pavement a mother shook her little boy. Two lovers held hands smiling. . . . And the blind man? Anna had lapsed into a mood of compassion which greatly distressed her.

She had skillfully pacified life; she had taken so much care to avoid upheavels. She had cultivated an atmosphere of serene understanding, separating each person from the others. Her clothes were clearly designed to be practical, and she could choose the evening's film from the newspaper—and everything was done in such a manner that each day should smoothly succeed the previous one. And a blind man chewing gum was destroying all this. Through her compassion Anna felt that life was filled to the brim with a sickening nausea.

Only then did she realize that she had passed her stop ages ago. In her weak state everything touched her with alarm. She got off the tram, her legs shaking, and looked around her, clutching the string bag stained with egg. For a moment she was unable to get her bearings. She seemed to have plunged into the middle of the night.

It was a long road, with high yellow walls. Her heart beat with fear as she tried in vain to recognize her surroundings; while the life she had discovered continued to pulsate, a gentler, more mysterious wind caressed her face. She stood quietly observing the wall. At last she recognized it. Advancing a little further alongside a hedge, she passed through the gates of the botanical garden.

She strolled wearily up the central avenue, between the palm trees. There was no one in the garden. She put her parcels down on the ground and sat down on the bench of a side path where she remained for some time.

The wilderness seemed to calm her, the silence regulating her breathing and soothing her senses.

From afar she saw the avenue where the evening was round and clear. But the shadows of the branches covered the side path.

Around her there were tranquil noises, the scent of trees, chance encounters among the creeping plants. The entire garden fragmented by the ever more fleeting moments of the evening. From whence came the drowsiness with which she was surrounded? As if induced by the drone of birds and bees. Everything seemed strange, much too gentle, much too great.

A gentle, familiar movement startled her and she turned round rapidly. Nothing appeared to have stirred. But in the central lane there stood, immobile, an enormous cat. Its fur was soft. With another silent movement, it disappeared.

Agitated, she looked about her. The branches swayed, their shadows wavering on the ground. A sparrow foraged in the soil. And suddenly, in terror, she imagined that she had fallen into an ambush. In the garden there was a secret activity in progress which she was beginning to penetrate.

On the trees, the fruits were black and sweet as honey. On the ground there lay dry fruit stones full of circumvolutions like small rotted cerebrums. The bench was stained with purple sap. With gentle persistence the waters murmured. On the tree trunk the luxurious feelers of parasites fastened themselves. The rawness of the world was peaceful. The murder was deep. And death was not what one had imagined.

As well as being imaginary, this was a world to be devoured with one's teeth, a world of voluminous dahlias and tulips. The trunks were pervaded by leafy parasites, their embrace soft and clinging. Like the resistance that precedes surrender, it was fascinating; the woman felt disgusted, and it was fascinating.

The trees were laden, and the world was so rich that it was rotting. When Anna reflected that there were children and grown men suffering hunger, the nausea reached her throat as if she were pregnant and abandoned. The moral of the garden was something different. Now that the blind man had guided her to it, she trembled on the threshold of a dark, fascinating world where monstrous water lilies floated. The small flowers scattered on the grass did not appear to be yellow or pink, but the color of inferior gold and scarlet. Their decay was profound, perfumed. But all these oppressive things she watched, her head surrounded by a swarm of insects, sent by some more refined life in the world. The breeze penetrated between the flowers. Anna imagined rather than felt its sweetened scent. The garden was so beautiful that she feared hell.

It was almost night now and everything seemed replete and heavy; a squirrel leapt in the darkness. Under her feet the earth was soft. Anna inhaled its odor with delight. It was both fascinating and repulsive.

But when she remembered the children, before whom she now felt guilty, she straightened up with a cry of pain. She clutched the package, advanced through the dark side path, and reached the avenue. She was almost running, and she saw the garden all around her aloof and impersonal. She shook the locked gates, and went on shaking them, gripping the rough timber. The watchman appeared, alarmed at not having seen her.

Until she reached the entrance of the building, she seemed to be on the brink of disaster. She ran with the string bag to the elevator, her heart beating in her breast—what was happening? Her compassion for the blind man was as fierce as anguish but the world seemed hers, dirty, perishable, hers. She opened the door of her flat. The room was large, square, the polished knobs were shining, the window panes were shining, the lamp shone brightly—what new land was this? And for a moment that wholesome life she had led until today seemed morally crazy. The little boy who came running up to embrace her was a creature with long legs and a face resembling her own. She pressed him firmly to her in anxiety and fear. Trembling, she protected herself. Life was vulnerable. She loved the world, she loved all things created, she loved with loathing. In the same way as she had always been fascinated by oysters, with that vague sentiment of revulsion which the approach of truth provoked, admonishing her. She embraced her son, almost hurting him. Almost as if she knew of some evil—the blind man or the beautiful botanical garden—she was clinging to him, to him whom she loved above all things. She had been touched by the demon of faith.

"Life is horrible," she said to him in a low voice, as if famished. What would she do if she answered the blind man's call? She would go alone. . . . There were poor and rich places that needed her. She needed them. "I am afraid", she said. She felt the delicate ribs of the child between her arms, she heard his frightened weeping.

"Mummy," the child called. She held him away from her, she studied his face and her heart shrank.

"Don't let Mummy forget you," she said. No sooner had the child felt her embrace weaken than he escaped and ran to the door of the room, from where he watched her more safely. It was the worst look that she had ever received. The blood rose hot to her cheeks.

She sank into a chair, with her fingers still clasping the string bag. What was she ashamed of? There was no way of escaping. The very crust of the days she had forged had broken and the water was escaping. She stood before the oysters. And there was no way of averting her gaze. What was she ashamed of? Certainly it was no longer pity, it was more than pity: her heart had filled with the worst will to live.

She no longer knew if she was on the side of the blind man or of the thick plants. The man little by little had moved away, and in her torment she appeared to have passed over to the side of those who had injured his eyes. The botanical garden, tranquil and high, had been a revelation. With horror, she discovered that she belonged to the strong part of the world, and what name should she give to her fierce compassion? Would she be obliged to kiss the leper, since she would never be just a sister. "A blind man has drawn me to the worst of myself," she thought, amazed. She felt herself banished because no pauper would drink water from her burning hands. Ah! It was easier to be a saint than a person! Good heavens, then was it not real, that pity which had fathomed the deepest waters in her heart? But it was the compassion of a lion.

Humiliated, she knew that the blind man would prefer a poorer love. And, trembling, she also knew why. The life of the botanical garden summoned her as a werewolf is summoned by the moonlight. "Oh! but she loved the blind man," she thought with tears in her eyes. Meanwhile it was not with this sentiment that one would go to church. "I am frightened," she whispered alone in the room. She got up and went to the kitchen to help the maid prepare dinner.

But life made her shiver like the cold of winter. She heard the school bell pealing, distant and constant. The small horror of the dust gathering in threads around the bottom of the stove, where she had discovered a small spider. Lifting a vase to change the water—there was the horror of the flower submitting itself, languid and loathsome, to her hands. The same secret activity was going on here in the kitchen. Near the waste bin, she crushed an ant with her foot. The small murder of the ant. Its minute body trembled. Drops of water fell on the stagnant water in the pool.

The summer beetles. The horror of those expressionless beetles. All around there was a silent, slow, insistent life. Horror upon horror. She went from one side of the kitchen to the other, cutting the steaks, mixing the cream. Circling around her head, around the light, the flies of a warm summer's evening. A night in which compassion was as crude as false love. Sweat trickled between her breasts. Faith broke her; the heat of the oven burned in her eyes.

Then her husband arrived, followed by her brothers and their wives, and her brothers' children.

They dined with all the windows open, on the ninth floor. An airplane shuddered menacingly in the heat of the sky. Although she had used few eggs, the dinner was good. The children stayed up, playing on the carpet with their cousins. It was summer and it would be useless to force them to go to sleep. Anna was a little pale and laughed gently with the others.

After dinner, the first cool breeze finally entered the room. The family was seated round the table, tired after their day, happy in the absence of any discord, eager not to find fault. They laughed at everything, with warmth and humanity. The children grew up admirably around them. Anna took the moment like a butterfly, between her fingers before it might escape forever.

Later, when they had all left and the children were in bed, she was just a woman looking out of the window. The city was asleep and warm. Would the experience unleashed by the blind man fill her days? How many years would it take before she once more grew old? The slightest movement on her part and she would trample one of her children. But with the ill-will of a lover, she seemed to accept that the fly would emerge from the flower, and the giant water lilies would float in the darkness of the lake. The blind man was hanging among the fruits of the botanical garden.

What if that were the stove exploding with the fire spreading through the house, she thought to herself as she ran to the kitchen where she found her husband in front of the spilt coffee.

"What happened?" she cried, shaking from head to foot. He was taken aback by his wife's alarm. And suddenly understanding, he laughed.

"It was nothing," he said, "I am just a clumsy fellow." He looked tired, with dark circles under his eyes.

But, confronted by the strange expression on Anna's face, he studied her more closely. Then he drew her to him in a sudden caress.

"I don't want anything ever to happen to you!" she said.

"You can't prevent the stove from having its little explosions," he replied, smiling. She remained limp in his arms. This afternoon, something tranquil had exploded, and in the house every-thing struck a tragicomic note.

"It's time to go to bed," he said, "it's late." In a gesture which was not his, but which seemed natural, he held his wife's hand, taking her with him, without looking back, removing her from the danger of living.

The giddiness of compassion had spent itself. And if she had crossed love and its hell, she was now combing her hair before the mirror, without any world for the moment in her heart. Before getting into bed, as if she were snuffing a candle, she blew out that day's tiny flame.

The Chicken

It was the chicken for Sunday's lunch. Still alive, because it was still only nine o'clock in the morning. She seemed placid enough. Since Saturday she had huddled in a corner of the kitchen. She looked at no one and no one paid any attention to her. Even when they had chosen the chicken, feeling the intimacy of her body with indifference, they could not tell if she were plump or thin. No one would ever have guessed that the chicken felt anxious.

It was a surprise, therefore, when they saw her spread open her stubby wings, puff out her breast, and in two or three attempts, fly to the backyard wall. She still hesitated for a second —sufficient time for the cook to cry out—and soon she was on their neighbor's terrace, from which, in another awkward flight, she reached the roof. There the chicken remained, like a displaced ornament, perched hesitantly now on one foot, now on the other. The family was hastily summoned and in consternation saw their lunch outlined against a chimney. The master of the house, reminding himself of the twofold necessity of sporadically engaging in sport and of getting the family some lunch, appeared resplendent in a pair of swimming trunks and resolved to follow the path traced by the chicken: in cautious leaps and bounds, he scaled the roof where the chicken, hesitant and tremulous, urgently decided on another route. The chase now intensified. From roof to roof, more than a block along the road was covered. Little accustomed to such a savage struggle for survival, the chicken had to decide for herself the paths she must follow without any assistance from her race. The man, however, was a natural hunter. And no matter how abject the prey, the cry of victory was in the air.

Alone in the world, without father or mother, the chicken was running and panting, dumb and intent. At times during her escape she hovered on some roof edge, gasping for breath and, while the man strenuously clambered up somewhere else, she had time to rest for a moment. And she seemed so free. Stupid, timid, and free. Not victorious as a cock would be in flight. What was it in the chicken's entrails that made her a *being*? The chicken is, in fact, a *being*. It is true that one would not be able to rely upon her for anything. Nor was she even self-reliant like the cock who believes in his crest. Her only advantage was that there were so many chickens that when one died, another automatically appeared, so similar in appearance that it might well be the same chicken.

Finally, on one of those occasions when she paused to enjoy her bid for freedom, the man reached her. Amid shrieks and feathers, she was caught. She was immediately carried off in triumph by one wing across the roof tiles and dumped somewhat violently on the kitchen floor. Still giddy, she shook herself a little with raucous and uncertain cackles.

It was then that it happened. Positively flustered, the chicken laid an egg. She was surprised and exhausted. Perhaps it was premature. But from the moment she was born, as if destined for motherhood, the chicken had shown all the signs of being instinctively maternal. She settled on the egg and there she remained, breathing as her eyes buttoned and unbuttoned. Her heart, which looked so tiny on a plate, raised and lowered her feathers, warming that egg which would never be anything else. Only the little girl of the house was on the scene, and she assisted at the event in utter dismay. No sooner had she disengaged herself from the event than she jumped up from the floor and ran out shouting.

"Mummy! Mummy! Don't kill the chicken, she's laid an egg! The chicken loves us!"

They all ran back into the kitchen and stood round the young mother in silence. Warming her offspring, she was neither gentle nor cross, neither happy nor sad; she was nothing, she was simply a chicken—a fact that did not suggest any particular feeling. The father, mother, and daughter had been standing there for some time now, without thinking about anything in particular. No one was known to have caressed a chicken on the head. Finally, the father decided, with a certain brusqueness, "If you have this chicken killed, I will never again eat a fowl as long as I live!"

"Nor me!" the little girl promised with passion.

The mother, feeling weary, shrugged her shoulders. Unconscious of the life that had been spared her, the chicken became part of the family. The little girl, upon returning from school, would toss her school bag down without disturbing the chicken's wanderings across the kitchen. The father, from time to time, still remembered. "And to think that I made her run in that state!"

The chicken became the queen of the household. Everybody, except her, knew it. She ran to and fro, from the kitchen to the terrace at the back of the house, exploiting her two sources of power: apathy and fear.

But when everyone was quiet in the house and seemed to have forgotten her, she puffed up with modest courage, the last traces of her great escape. She circled the tiled floor, her body advancing behind her head, as unhurried as if in an open field, although her small head betrayed her, darting back and forth in rapid vibrant movements, with the age-old fear of her species now ingrained. Once in a while, but ever more infrequently, she remembered how she had stood out against the sky on the roof edge ready to cry out. At such moments, she filled her lungs with the stuffy atmosphere of the kitchen and, had females been given the power to crow, she would not have crowed but would have felt much happier. Not even at those moments, however, did the expression on her empty head alter. In flight or in repose, when she gave birth or while pecking grain, hers was a chicken's head, identical to that drawn at the beginning of time. Until one day they killed her and ate her, and the years rolled on.

The Imitation of the Rose

Before Armando came home from work the house would have to be tidied and Laura herself ready in her brown dress so that she could attend her husband while he dressed, and then they would leave at their leisure, arm in arm as in former times. How long was it since they had last done that?

But now that she was "well" again, they would take the bus, she looking like a wife, watching out of the bus window, her arm in his: and later they would dine with Carlota and João, sitting back intimately in their chairs. How long was it since she had seen Armando sit back with intimacy and converse with another man? A man at peace was one who, oblivious of his wife's presence, could converse with another man about the latest news in the headlines. Meantime, she would talk to Carlota about women's things, submissive to the authoritarian and practical goodness of Carlota, receiving once more her friend's attention and vague disdain, her natural abruptness, instead of that perplexed affection full of curiosity—watching Armando, finally oblivious of his own wife. And she herself, finally returning to play an insignificant role with gratitude. Like a cat which, having spent the night out of doors, as if nothing had happened, had unexpectedly found a saucer of milk waiting. People fortunately helped to make her feel that she was "well" again. Without watching her, they actively helped her to forget, they themselves feigning forgetfulness as if they had read the same directions on the same medicine bottle. Or, perhaps, they had really forgotten. How long was it since she last saw Armando sit back with abandon, oblivious of her presence? And she herself?

Interrupting her efforts to tidy up the dressing table, Laura gazed at herself in the mirror. And she herself? How long had it been? Her face had a domestic charm, her hair pinned behind her large pale ears. Her brown eyes and brown hair, her soft dark skin, all lent to that face, no longer so very young, the unassuming expression of a woman. Perhaps someone might have seen in that ever so tiny hint of surprise in the depths of her eyes, perhaps someone might have seen in that ever so tiny hint of sorrow the lack of children which she never had?

With her punctilious liking for organization—that same inclination which had made her as a school-girl copy out her class notes in perfect writing without ever understanding them—to tidy up the house before the maid had her afternoon off so that, once Maria went out, she would have nothing more to do except (1) calmly get dressed; (2) wait for Armando once she was ready; (3) what was the third thing? Ah yes. That was exactly what she would do. She would wear her brown dress with the cream lace collar. Having already had her bath. Even during her time at the Sacred Heart Convent she had always been tidy and clean, with an obsession for personal hygiene and a certain horror of disorder. A fact which never caused Carlota, who was already a little odd even as a school girl, to admire her. The reactions of the two women had always been different. Carlota, ambitious and laughing heartily; Laura, a little slow, and virtually always taking care to be slow. Carlota, seeing danger in nothing; and Laura ever cautious. When they had given her *The Imitation of Christ* to read, with the zeal of a donkey she had read the book without understanding it, but may God forgive her, she had felt that anyone who imitated Christ would be lost—lost in the light, but dangerously lost. Christ was the worst temptation. And Carlota, who had not even attempted to read it, had lied to the Sister, saying that she had finished it.

That was decided. She would wear her brown dress with the cream collar made of real lace.

But when she saw the time, she remembered with alarm, causing her to raise her hand to her breast, that she had forgotten to drink her glass of milk.

She made straight for the kitchen and, as if she had guiltily betrayed Armando and their devoted friends through her neglect, standing by the refrigerator she took the first sips with anxious pauses, concentrating upon each sip with faith as if she were compensating everyone and showing her repentance.

If the doctor had said, "Take milk between your meals, and avoid an empty stomach because that causes anxiety," then, even without the threat of anxiety, she took her milk without further discussion, sip by sip, day by day—she never failed, obeying blindly with a touch of zeal, so that she might not perceive in herself the slightest disbelief. The embarrassing thing was that the doctor appeared to contradict himself, for while giving precise instructions that she chose to follow with the zeal of a convert, he had also said, "Relax! Take things easy; don't force yourself to succeed—completely forget what has happened and everything will return to normal." And he had given her a pat on the back that had pleased her and made her blush with pleasure.

But in her humble opinion, the one command seemed to cancel out the other, as if they were asking her to eat flour and whistle at the same time. In order to fuse both commands into one, she had invented a solution: that glass of milk which had finished up by gaining a secret power, which almost embodied with every sip the taste of a word and renewed that firm pat on the back, that glass of milk she carried into the sitting room where she sat "with great naturalness," feigning a lack of interest, "not forcing herself"—and thereby cleverly complying with the second order. It doesn't matter if I get fat, she thought, beauty has never been the most important thing.

She sat down on the couch as if she were a guest in her own home, which, so recently regained, tidy and impersonal, recalled the peace of a stranger's house. A feeling that gave her great satisfaction: the opposite of Carlota who had made of her home something similar to herself. Laura experienced such pleasure in making something impersonal of her home; in a certain way perfect, because impersonal.

Oh, how good it was to be back, to be truly back, she smiled with satisfaction. Holding the almost empty glass, she closed her eyes with a pleasurable weariness. She had ironed Armando's shirts, she had prepared methodical lists for the following day, she had calculated in detail what she had spent at the market that morning; she had not paused, in fact, for a single minute. Oh, how good it was to be tired again!

If some perfect creature were to descend from the planet Mars and discover that people on the Earth were tired and growing old, he would feel pity and dismay. Without ever understanding what was good about being people, about feeling tired and failing daily; only the initiated would understand this nuance of depravity and refinement of life.

And she had returned at last from the perfection of the planet Mars. She, who had never had any ambitions except to be a wife to some man, gratefully returned to find her share of what is daily fallible. With her eyes closed she sighed gratefully. How long was it since she had felt tired? But now every day she felt almost exhausted. She had ironed, for example, Armando's shirts; she had always enjoyed ironing and, modesty aside, she pressed clothes to perfection. And afterward she felt exhausted as a sort of compensation. No longer to feel that alert lack of fatigue. No longer to feel that point—empty, aroused, and hideously exhilarating within oneself. No longer to feel that terrible independence. No longer that monstrous and simple facility of not sleeping—neither by day nor by night—which in her discretion had suddenly made her superhuman by comparison with her tired and perplexed husband. Armando, with that offensive breath which he developed when he was silently preoccupied, stirring in her a poignant compassion, yes, even within her alert perfection, her feeling and love . . . she, superhuman and tranquil in her bright isolation, and he—when he had come to visit her timidly bringing apples and grapes that the nurse, with a shrug of her shoulders, used to eat—he visiting her ceremoniously like a lover with heavy breath and fixed smile, forcing himself in his heroism to try to understand . . . he who had received her from a father and a clergyman, and who did not know what to do with this girl from Tijuca, who unexpectedly, like a tranquil boat spreading its sails over the waters, had become superhuman.

But now it was over. All over. Oh, it had been a mere weakness: temperament was the worst temptation. But later she had recovered so completely that she had even started once more to exercise care not to plague others with her former obsession for detail. She could well remember her companions at the convent saying to her, "That's the thousandth time you've counted that!" She remembered them with an uneasy smile.

She had recovered completely: now she was tired every day, every day her face sagged as the afternoon wore on, and the night then assumed its old finality and became more than just a perfect starry night. And everything completed itself harmoniously. And, as for the whole world, each day fatigued her; as for the whole world, human and perishable. No longer did she feel that perfection or youth. No longer that thing which one day had clearly spread like a cancer . . . her soul.

She opened her eyes heavy with sleep, feeling the consoling solidity of the glass in her hand, but closed them again with a comfortable smile of fatigue, bathing herself like a *nouveau riche* in all his wealth, in this familiar and slightly nauseating water. Yes, slightly nauseating: what did it matter?. For if she, too, was a little nauseating, she was fully aware of it. But her husband didn't think so and then what did it matter, for happily she did not live in surroundings which demanded that she should be more clever and interesting, she was even free of school which so embarrassingly had demanded that she should be alert. What did it matter? In exhaustion—she had ironed Armando's shirts without mentioning that she had been to the market in the morning and had spent some time there with that delight she took in making things yield—in exhaustion she found a refuge, that discreet and obscure place from where, with so much constraint toward herself and others, she had once departed. But as she was saying, fortunately she had returned.

And if she searched with greater faith and love she would find within her exhaustion that even better place, which would be sleep. She sighed with pleasure, for one moment of mischievous malice tempted to go against that warm breath she exhaled, already inducing sleep . . . for one moment tempted to doze off. "Just for a moment, only one tiny moment!" she pleaded with herself, pleased at being so tired, she pleaded persuasively, as one pleads with a man, a facet of her behavior that had always delighted Armando. But she did not really have time to sleep now, not even to take a nap, she thought smugly and with false modesty. She was such a busy person! She had always envied those who could say "I couldn't find the time," and now once more she was such a busy person.

They were going to dinner at Carlota's house, and everything had to be organized and ready, it was her first dinner out since her return and she did not wish to arrive late, she had to be ready. "Well, I've already said this a thousand times," she thought with embarrassment. It would be sufficient to say it only once. "I did not wish to arrive late." For this was a sufficient reason: if she had never been able to bear without enormous vexation giving trouble to anyone, now more than ever, she should not. No, no, there was not the slightest doubt: she had no time to sleep. What she must do, stirring herself with familiarity in that intimate wealth of routine—and it hurt her that Carlota should despise her liking for routine—what she must do was (1) wait until the maid was ready; (2) give her the money so that she could bring the meat in the morning, top round of beef; how could she explain that the difficulty of finding good meat was, for her, really an interesting topic of conversation, but if Carlota were to find out, she would despise her; (3) to begin washing and dressing herself carefully, surrendering, without reservations to the pleasure of making the most of the time at her disposal. Her brown dress matched her eyes, and her collar in cream lace gave her an almost childlike appearance, like some child from the past. And, back in the nocturnal peace of Tijuca, no longer that dazzling light of ebullient nurses, their hair carefully set, going out to enjoy themselves after having tossed her like a helpless chicken into the void of insulin—back to the nocturnal peace of Tijuca, restored to her real life.

She would go out arm in arm with Armando, walking slowly to the bus stop with those low thick hips which her girdle parceled into one, transforming her into a striking woman. But when she awkwardly explained to Armando that this resulted from ovarian insufficiency, Armando, who liked his wife's hips, would saucily retort, "What good would it do me to be married to a ballerina?" That was how he responded. No one would have suspected it, but at times Armando could be extremely devious. From time to time they repeated the same phrases. She explained that it was on account of ovarian insufficiency. Then he would retort, "What good would it do me to be married to a ballerina?" At times he was shameless and no one would have suspected it.

Carlota would have been horrified if she were to know that they, too, had an intimate life and shared things she could not discuss, but nevertheless she regretted not being able to discuss them. Carlota certainly thought that she was only neat and ordinary and a little boring; but if she were obliged to take care in order not to annoy the others with details, with Armando she let herself go at times and became boring. Not that this mattered because, although he pretended to listen, he did not absorb everything she told him. Nor did she take offense, because she understood perfectly well that her conversation rather bored other people, but it was nice to be able to tell him that she had been able to find good meat, even if Armando shook his head and did not listen. She and the maid conversed a great deal, in fact more so she than the maid, and she was careful not to bother the maid, who at times suppressed her impatience and became somewhat rude—the fault was really hers because she did not always command respect.

But, as she was saying . . . her arm in his, she short and he tall and thin, though he was healthy, thank God, and she was chestnut-haired. Chestnut-haired as she obscurely felt a wife ought to be. To have black or blonde hair was an exaggeration, which, in her desire to make the right choice, she had never wanted. Then, as for green eyes, it seemed to her that if she had green eyes it would be as if she had not told her husband everything. Not that Carlota had given cause for any scandal, although Laura, were she given the opportunity, would hotly defend her, but the opportunity had never arisen. She, Laura, was obliged reluctantly to agree that her friend had a strange and amusing manner of treating her husband, not because "they treated each other as equals," since this was now common enough, but you know what I mean to say. And Carlota was even a little different, even she had remarked on this once to Armando and Armando had agreed without attaching much importance to the fact. But, as she was saying, in brown with the lace collar . . . her reverie filled her with the same pleasure she experienced when tidying out drawers, and she even found herself disarranging them in order to tidy them up again.

She opened her eyes and, as if it were the room that had taken a nap and not she, the room seemed refurbished and refreshed with its chairs brushed and its curtains, which had shrunk in the last washing, looking like trousers that are too short and the wearer looking comically at his own legs. Oh! how good it was to see everything tidy again and free of dust, everything cleaned by her own capable hands, and so silent and with a vase of flowers as in a waiting room. She had always found waiting rooms pleasing, so respectful and impersonal. How satisfying life together was, for her who had at last returned from extravagance. Even a vase of flowers. She looked at it.

"Ah! how lovely they are," her heart exclaimed suddenly, a bit childish. They were small wild roses which she had bought that morning at the market, partly because the man had insisted so much, partly out of daring. She had arranged them in a vase that very morning, while drinking her sacred glass of milk at ten o'clock.

But in the light of this room the roses stood in all their complete and tranquil beauty. "I have never seen such lovely roses," she thought enquiringly. And, as if she had not just been thinking precisely this, vaguely aware that she had been thinking precisely this, and quickly dismissing her embarrassment upon recognizing herself as being a little tedious, she thought in a newer phase of surprise, "Really, I have never seen such pretty roses." She looked at them attentively. But her attention could not be sustained for very long as simple attention, and soon transformed itself into soothing pleasure, and she was no longer able to analyze the roses and felt obliged to interrupt herself with the same exclamation of submissive enquiry: "How lovely they are!"

They were a bouquet of perfect roses, several on the same stem. At some moment they had climbed with quick eagerness over each other but then, their game over, they had become tranquilly immobilized. They were quite perfect roses in their minuteness, not quite open, and their pink hue was almost white. "They seem almost artificial," she uttered in surprise. They might give the impression of being white if they were completely open, but with the center petals curled in a bud, their color was concentrated and, as in the lobe of an ear, one could sense the redness circulate inside them. "How lovely they are," thought Laura, surprised. But without knowing why, she felt somewhat restrained and a little perplexed. Oh, nothing serious, it was only that such extreme beauty disturbed her.

She heard the maid's footsteps on the brick floor of the kitchen, and from the hollow sound she realized that she was wearing high heels and that she must be ready to leave. Then Laura had an idea which was in some way highly original: why not ask Maria to call at Carlota's house and leave the roses as a present?

And also because that extreme beauty disturbed her. Disturbed her? It was a risk. Oh! no, why a risk? It merely disturbed her; they were a warning. Oh! no, why a warning? Maria would deliver the roses to Carlota.

"Dona Laura sent them," Maria would say. She smiled thoughtfully: Carlota would be puzzled that Laura, being able to bring the roses personally, since she wanted to present them to her, should send them before dinner with the maid. Not to mention that she would find it amusing to receive the roses . . . and would think it "refined."

"These things aren't necessary between us, Laura!" the other would say with that frankness of hers which was somewhat tactless, and Laura would exclaim in a subdued cry of rapture, "Oh, no! no! It is not because of the invitation to dinner! It is because the roses are so lovely that I felt the impulse to give them to you!"

Yes, if at the time the opportunity arose and she had the courage, that was exactly what she would say. What exactly would she say? It was important not to forget. She would say, "Oh, no! no! It is not because of the invitation to dinner! It is because the roses are so lovely that I felt the impulse to give them to you!"

And Carlota would be surprised at the delicacy of Laura's sentiments—no one would imagine that Laura, too, had her ideas. In this imaginary and pleasurable scene which made her smile devoutly, she addressed herself as "Laura," as if speaking to a third person. A third person full of that gentle, rustling, pleasant, and tranquil faith, Laura, the one with the real lace collar, dressed discreetly, the wife of Armando, an Armando, after all, who no longer needed to force himself to pay attention to all of her conversation about the maid and the meat . . . who no longer needed to think about his wife, like a man who is happy, like a man who is not married to a ballerina.

"I couldn't help sending you the roses," Laura would say, this third person so, but so. . . . And to give the roses was almost as nice as the roses themselves.

And she would even be rid of them.

And what exactly would happen next? Ah yes; as she was

saying, Carlota, surprised at Laura who was neither intelligent nor good but who had her secret feelings. And Armando? Armando would look at her with a look of real surprise—for it was essential to remember that he must not know the maid had taken the roses in the afternoon! Armando would look with kindness upon the impulses of his little wife and that night they would sleep together.

And she would have forgotten the roses and their beauty. No, she suddenly thought, vaguely warned. It was necessary to take care with that alarmed look in others. It was necessary never to cause them alarm, especially with everything being so fresh in their minds. And, above all, to spare everyone the least anxiety or doubt. And that the attention of others should no longer be necessary—no longer this horrible feeling of their watching her in silence, and her in their presence. No more impulses.

But at the same time she saw the empty glass in her hand and she also thought, " 'He' said that I should not force myself to succeed, that I should not think of adopting attitudes merely to show that I am."

"Maria," she called, upon hearing the maid's footsteps once more. And when Maria appeared she asked with a note of rashness and defiance, "Would you call at Dona Carlota's house and leave these roses for her? Just say that Dona Laura sent them. Just say it like that. Dona Laura. . . ."

"Yes, I know," the maid interrupted her patiently.

Laura went to search for an old sheet of tissue paper. Then she carefully lifted the roses from the vase, so lovely and tranquil, with their delicate and mortal thorns. She wanted to make a really artistic bouquet: and at the same time she would be rid of them. And she would be able to dress and resume her day. When she had arranged the moist blooms in a bouquet, she held the flowers away from her and examined them at a distance, slanting her head and half-closing her eyes for an impartial and severe judgment.

And when she looked at them, she saw the roses. And then, irresistibly gentle, she insinuated to herself, "Don't give the roses away, they are so lovely."

A second later, still very gentle, her thought suddenly became slightly more intense, almost tempting, "Don't give them away, they are yours." Laura became a little frightened: because things were never hers.

But these roses were. Rosy, small, and perfect: they were hers. She looked at them, incredulous: they were beautiful and they were hers. If she could think further ahead, she would think: hers as nothing before now had ever been.

And she could even keep them because that initial uneasiness had passed which had caused her vaguely to avoid looking at the roses too much.

"Why give them away then? They are so lovely and you are giving them away? So when you find something nice, you just go and give it away? Well, if they were hers," she insinuated persuasively to herself, without finding any other argument beyond the previous one which, when repeated, seemed to her to be ever more convincing and straightforward.

"They would not last long—why give them away then, so long as they were alive?" The pleasure of possessing them did not represent any great risk, she pretended to herself, because, whether she liked it or not, shortly she would be forced to deprive herself of them and then she would no longer think about them, because by then they would have withered.

"They would not last long; why give them away then?" The fact that they would not last long seemed to free her from the guilt of keeping them, in the obscure logic of the woman who sins. Well, one could see that they would not last long (it would be sudden, without danger). And it was not even, she argued in a final and victorious rejection of guilt, she herself who had wanted to buy them; the flower seller had insisted so much and she always became so intimidated when they argued with her. ... It was not she who had wanted to buy them ... she was not to blame in the slightest. She looked at them in rapture, thoughtful and profound.

"And, honestly, I never saw such perfection in all my life."

All right, but she had already spoken to Maria and there would be no way of turning back. Was it too late then? She became frightened upon seeing the tiny roses that waited impassively in her own hand. If she wanted, it would not be too late. . . . She could say to Maria, "Oh Maria, I have decided to take the roses myself when I go to dinner this evening!" And of course she would not take them. . . . And Maria need never know. And, before changing, she would sit on the couch for a moment, just for a moment, to contemplate them. To contemplate that tranquil impassivity of the roses. Yes, because having already done the deed, it would be better to profit from it . . . she would not be foolish enough to take the blame without the profit. That was exactly what she would do.

But with the roses unwrapped in her hand she waited. She did not arrange them in the vase, nor did she call Maria. She knew why. Because she must give them away. Oh, she knew why.

And also because something nice was either for giving or receiving, not only for possessing. And above all, never for one *to be.* Above all, one should never *be* a lovely thing. A lovely thing lacked the gesture of giving. One should never keep a lovely thing, as if it were guarded within the perfect silence of one's heart. (Although, if she were not to give the roses, would anyone ever find out? It was horribly easy and within one's reach to keep them, for who would find out? And they would be hers, and things would stay as they were and the matter would be forgotten. . .)

"Well then? Well then?" she mused, vaguely disturbed.

Well, no. What she must do was to wrap them up and send them, without any pleasure now; to parcel them up and, disappointed, send them; and, terrified, be rid of them. Also, because a person had to be coherent, one's thoughts had to be consistent: if, spontaneously, she had decided to relinquish them to Carlota, she should stand by that decision and give them away. For no one changed their mind from one minute to another.

But anyone can repent, she suddenly rebelled. For if it was only the minute I took hold of the roses that I noticed how lovely they were, for the first time, actually, as I held them, I noticed how lovely they were. Or a little before that? (And they were really hers.) And even the doctor himself had patted her on the back and said, "Don't force yourself into pretending that you are well, because you *are* well!" And then that hearty pat on the back. So she was not obliged, therefore, to be consistent, she didn't have to prove anything to anyone, and she would keep the roses. (And in all sincerity—in all sincerity they were hers.)

"Are they ready?" Maria asked.

"Yes," said Laura, surprised.

She looked at them, so mute in her hand. Impersonal in their extreme beauty. In their extreme and perfect tranquillity as roses. That final instance: the flower. That final perfection; its luminous tranquillity.

Like someone depraved, she watched with vague longing the tempting perfection of the roses . . . with her mouth a little dry, she watched them.

Until, slowly, austerely, she wrapped the stems and thorns in the tissue paper. She was so absorbed that only upon holding out the bouquet she had prepared did she notice that Maria was no longer in the room—and she remained alone with her heroic sacrifice.

Vacantly, sorrowfully, she watched them, distant as they were at the end of her outstretched arm—and her mouth became even dryer, parched by that envy and desire.

"But they are mine," she said with enormous timidity.

When Maria returned and took hold of the bouquet, for one tiny moment of greed Laura drew back her hand, keeping the roses to herself for one more second—they are so lovely and they are mine—the first lovely thing and mine! And it was the flower seller who had insisted. . . . I did not go looking for them! It was destiny that had decreed! Oh, only this once! Only this once and I swear never more! (She could at least take one rose for herself, no more than this! One rose for herself. And only she would know and then never more; oh, she promised herself that never more would she allow herself to be tempted by perfection, never more.)

And the next moment, without any transition, without any obstacle, the roses were in the maid's hand, they were no longer hers, like a letter already in the post! One can no longer recover or obliterate statements! There is no point in shouting, "That was not what I wanted to say!" Her hands were now empty but her heart, obstinate and resentful, was still saying, "You can catch Maria on the stairs, you know perfectly well that you can, and take the roses from her hand and steal them—because to take them now would be to steal them." To steal what was hers? For this was what a person without any feeling for others would do: he would steal what was his by right! Have pity, dear God. You can get them back, she insisted, enraged. And then the front door slammed.

Slowly, she sat down calmly on the couch. Without leaning back. Only to rest. No, she was no longer angry, not even a little. But that tiny wounded spot in the depths of her eyes was larger and thoughtful. She looked at the vase.

"Where are my roses?" she said then very quietly.

And she missed the roses. They had left an empty space inside her. Remove an object from a clean table and by the cleaner patch which remains one sees that there has been dust all around it. The roses had left a patch without dust and without sleep inside her. In her heart, that one rose, which at least she could have taken for herself without prejudicing anyone in the world, was gone. Like something missing. Indeed, like some great loss. An absence that flooded into her like a light. And also around the mark left by the roses the dust was disappearing. The center of fatigue opened itself into a circle that grew larger. As if she had not ironed a single shirt for Armando. And in the clearing they had left, one missed those roses.

"Where are my roses?" she moaned without pain, smoothing the pleats of her skirt.

Like lemon juice dripping into dark tea and the dark tea becoming completely clear, her exhaustion gradually became clearer. Without, however, any tiredness. Just as the firefly alights. Since she was no longer tired, she was on the point of getting up to dress. It was time to start getting ready.

With parched lips, she tried for an instant to imitate the roses deep down inside herself. It was not even difficult.

It was just as well that she did not feel tired. In this way she would go out to dinner feeling more refreshed. Why not wear her cameo brooch on her cream-colored collar? The one the Major had brought back from the war in Italy. It would add a final touch to her neckline. When she was ready she would hear the noise of Armando's key in the door. She must get dressed. But it was still early. With the rush-hour traffic, he would be late in arriving. It was still afternoon. An extremely beautiful afternoon. But, in fact, it was no longer afternoon. It was evening. From the street there arose the first sounds of darkness and the first lights.

Moreover, the key penetrated with familiarity the keyhole.

Armando would open the door. He would press the light switch. And suddenly in the frame of the doorway that face would appear, betraying an expectancy he tried to conceal but could not restrain. Then his breathless suspense would finally transform itself into a smile of utter relief. That embarrassed smile of relief which he would never suspect her of noticing.

That relief which, probably with a pat on the back, they had advised her poor husband to conceal. But which had been, for this woman whose heart was filled with guilt, her daily recompense for having restored to her husband the possibility of happiness and peace, sanctified at the hands of an austere priest who only permitted submissive happiness to humans and not the imitation of Christ.

The key turned in the lock, that dark, expectant face entered, and a powerful light flooded the room.

And in the doorway, Armando himself stopped short with that breathless expression as if he had run for miles in order to arrive in time. She was about to smile. So that she might dispel the anxious expectancy on his face, which always came mixed with the childish victory of having arrived in time to find his boring, good-hearted, and diligent wife. She was about to smile so that once more he might know that there would no longer be any danger in his arriving too late. She was about to smile in order to teach him gently to confide in her. It had been useless to advise them never to touch on the subject: they did not speak about it but they had created a language of facial expressions whereby fear and confidence were communicated, and question and answer were silently telegraphed. She was about to smile. She was taking her time, but meant to smile.

Calmly and sweetly she said, "It came back, Armando. It came back."

As if he would never understand, he averted his smiling, distrusting face. His main task for the moment was to try and control his breathless gasps after running up the stairs, now that, triumphantly, he had arrived in time, now that she was there to smile at him. As if he would never understand.

"What came back?" he finally asked her in an expressionless tone.

But while he was seeking never to understand, the man's face, ever more full of suspense, had already understood with-

out a single feature having altered. His main task was to gain
time and to concentrate upon controlling his breath. Which
suddenly was no longer difficult. For unexpectedly he noticed
to his horror that the room and the woman were calm and
showing no signs of haste. Still more suspicious, like someone
about to end up howling with laughter upon observing something absurd, he meantime insisted upon keeping his face
averted, from where he spied her cautiously, almost her enemy.
And from where he already began to feel unable to restrain
himself, from seeing her seated with her hands folded on her
lap, with the serenity of the firefly that is alight.

In her innocent, chestnut gaze, the embarrassed vanity of not
having been able to resist.

"What came back?" he asked suddenly with severity.

"I couldn't help myself," she said and her final compassion
for this man was in her voice, one last appeal for pardon which
already came mingled with the arrogance of an almost perfect
solitude.

"I couldn't prevent it," she repeated, surrendering to him with
relief the compassion which she with some effort had been able
to contain until he arrived.

"It was on account of the roses," she said modestly.

As if a photograph were about to capture that moment, he
still maintained the same disinterested expression, as if the
photographer had asked him only for his face and not his soul.
He opened his mouth and involuntarily his face took on for an
instant an expression of comic detachment which he had used
to conceal his annoyance when he had asked his boss for an in-
crease in salary. The next moment, he averted his eyes, mortified by his wife's shamelessness as she sat there unburdened
and serene.

But suddenly the tension fell. His shoulders dropped, the
features of his face relaxed and a great heaviness settled over
him. Aged and strange, he watched her.

She was seated wearing her little housedress. He knew that she had done everything possible not to become luminous and remote. With fear and respect he watched her. Aged, tired, and strange. But he did not even have a word to offer. From the open door he saw his wife sitting upright on the couch, once more alert and tranquil as if on a train. A train that had already departed.

Happy Birthday

The family gradually began to arrive. Those who had made the journey from Olaria were all dressed up because the visit also meant an outing to Copacabana. The daughter-in-law from Olaria wore a navy-blue dress trimmed with *pailletes* and a drape in front which disguised the fact that she was not wearing a girdle. Her husband had not accompanied her for one obvious reason: he did not want to meet his brothers and sister. But he had sent his wife so that the family ties should not be completely broken. And she had come in her best dress to show them that she could do without them, bringing her three children: two girls whose breasts were already taking form, dolled up like infants in pink ruffles and starched petticoats, and a little boy who looked self-conscious in his new suit and tie.

Zilda—the daughter with whom the old lady celebrating her birthday lived—had placed chairs all along the walls as if it were a party with dancing to follow. And after greeting everyone with a scowl on her face, the daughter-in-law from Olaria parked herself in one of the chairs and said not another word, her mouth pouting with displeasure and determined to play the role of martyr. "I only came for appearances sake," she had assured Zilda before sitting down immediately and looking offended. The two little girls in pink and the boy, with their yellow faces and their neatly combed hair, did not quite know what attitude to assume and they remained standing beside their mother, impressed by her navy-blue dress and its *pailletes*.

Next the daughter-in-law from Ipanema arrived with two grandsons and their nursemaid. Her husband would come later. And since Zilda—the only daughter in that large family where the other five were male, and the only one, it was decided years ago, who had the time and space to look after the old woman— was in the kitchen helping the maid put the finishing touches to the croquettes and sandwiches, they all just stood there: the daughter-in-law from Olaria sitting erect and haughty with her apprehensive children beside her, the daughter-in-law from Ipanema on the opposite row of chairs pretending to busy herself with the baby in order to avoid having to confront her brother-in-law's wife from Olaria, the nursemaid in her uniform, idle, with her mouth open.

And at the head of the long table sat the old woman for whom the party was being held to celebrate her eighty-ninth birthday.

Zilda, the mistress of the house, had laid the table early. She had arranged the inevitable colored paper napkins and disposable cups for the party; she had scattered balloons throughout the room, which were dangling from the ceiling, and on some of them was written *Happy Birthday*, on others *Feliz Aniversário*. In the center of the table stood an enormous cake covered with icing. In order to speed up the preparations, Zilda had decorated the table immediately after lunch, placed the chairs against the wall, and sent the children to play next door so that they wouldn't interfere with the table.

And, also in order to speed up the preparations, she had dressed the old lady immediately after lunch. She had fastened her chain round her neck and, pinning her brooch in position, she had then sprayed her with a little cologne to hide the musty smell—before seating her at the head of the table. And since two o'clock the old lady had been seated at the head of that long, empty table, rigid and upright in the silent room.

From time to time she was conscious of the colored napkins. She looked inquisitively as one or other of the balloons started to shake with the vibration of the passing traffic. And from time to time that mute anguish, when her gaze accompanied, fascinated and impotent, the flight of some fly around her cake. And there she remained waiting until four o'clock when her daughter-in-law from Olaria had arrived, followed by the one from Ipanema.

When the daughter-in-law from Ipanema felt that she could not endure another second of being seated in front of her brother-in-law's wife from Olaria, who, full of past offenses, could see no reason for averting her challenging gaze from the daughter-in-law from Ipanema—at long last José arrived with his family. And no sooner had they kissed each other than the room filled up with people who greeted each other noisily as if they had been waiting below for the moment to race up the three flights of stairs, in one last-minute scurry, chattering, dragging their startled children behind them, cramming into the room—and making a start to the party.

The muscles of the old woman's face no longer betrayed any expression, so that no one could tell if she was feeling happy. There she was stationed at the head of the table—an imposing old woman, large, gaunt, and dark. She looked almost hollow.

"Eighty-nine today, my word!" said José, the oldest of her

children now that Jonga had died. "Eighty-nine today, my word!" he said, rubbing his hands in public admiration and as an imperceptible sign to the others.

Everyone paused attentively and turned to gaze upon the old lady, who was celebrating her birthday in a more formal manner. Some shook their heads in wonder as if admiring some new record. Each year the old woman survived vaguely represented another stage in the whole family's progress.

"My word!" some repeated, smiling shyly.

"Eighty-nine years," echoed Emmanuel, who was José's partner. "She's only a youngster!" he said jokingly and nervous, and everybody laughed with the exception of his wife.

The old lady showed no reaction.

Some of the guests had not brought her a present. Others brought a soap dish, a woollen underset, a fancy brooch, and a small pot of cactus—nothing, absolutely nothing that the mistress of the house might be able to use for herself or her children, nothing that the old lady herself could really use or save on. The mistress of the house took charge of the presents, feeling bitter and ironic.

"Eighty-nine!" repeated a distressed Emmanuel as he looked at his wife.

But the old lady showed no reaction.

Then, as if they had all had the final proof that it was useless to force themselves further, with a shrug of their shoulders, as if they were dealing with a deaf-mute, they continued to enjoy the party by themselves, and started on the first helping of ham sandwiches, more as a proof of their enthusiasm than because they felt any appetite—despite their joking comments that they were dying of hunger. The punch was served, and Zilda was perspiring. None of her sisters-in-law really made any effort whatsoever to help. The warm fat of the croquettes made the room smell like an outdoor picnic, and, with their backs turned to the old lady, who was not allowed to eat fried things, they laughed apprehensively.

And what about Cordelia? Cordelia, the youngest daughter-in-law, was seated and smiling.

"No sir!" José retorted with feigned severity. "This is no day for talking business!"

"All right, all right then!" Emmanuel quickly withdrew, furtively glancing toward his wife, who from afar was listening attentively.

"We'll have no talk about business today," shouted José, "this is Mother's birthday."

At the head of the table, which was already stained, the cups dirty, and only the cake intact, there was the mother they discussed. The old lady blinked her eyes.

When the table was reduced to a mess, the nerves of the mothers on edge with the din their children were making, and the old granny sitting back complacently in her chair, they decided to put out the unnecessary light in the passage and light the solitary candle on the cake, a large candle with a piece of paper attached on which "89" was written.

But no one congratulated Zilda on her decoration, and she worriedly asked herself if they were not perhaps thinking that the idea was to economize on candles. No one seemed to remember that they had not even contributed as much as a box of matches toward the party and that she, Zilda, was serving them like a slave, her feet exhausted and her heart rebellious. Then they lit the candle. And José, their leader, sang with great force, encouraging those who hesitated or looked surprised with an authoritative look. "Off we go, all together now!" And they all suddenly began to sing aloud like soldiers. Roused by their voices, Cordelia watched them breathlessly. Since they had not agreed upon anything, some sang in Portuguese and others in English. They then tried to correct themselves: those who had been singing in English broke into Portuguese and those who had been singing in Portuguese started to sing very softly in English.

While they sang, the old lady meditated by the light of the candle, as if she were sitting by the fireside.

They chose the smallest of the great-grandchildren, who sat on his mother's lap, and after some persuasion he blew out the flame with one puff full of saliva. For a second they applauded the unexpected strength of the child, who, startled and triumphant, looked at everybody in sheer delight. The mistress of the house waited with her finger poised on the light switch in the passage and put on the light.

"Long live mother!"

"Long live granny!"

"Long live Anita!" said the next-door neighbor who had joined them.

"Happy birthday!" chanted her grandchildren from Bennett School.

A few half-hearted claps broke out again.

The old lady looked at her cake with its extinguished candle, and it now seemed big and dry.

"Cut your cake, granny!" said the mother of the four children. "She must cut her own cake!" she assured everyone hesitantly, with an air of intimacy and intrigue. And since they all approved, satisfied and curious, she suddenly became impetuous. "Cut your cake, granny!"

And, unexpectedly, the old lady grabbed the knife. And without hesitation, as if by hesitating for a second she might fall on her face, she dealt the first stroke with the grip of a murderess.

"Such strength," whispered the daughter-in-law from Ipanema, and one could not tell if she was shocked or agreeably surprised. She felt somewhat horrified.

"Only a year ago she could climb those stairs with more wind than I have," Zilda said bitterly.

The first cut having been made, as if the first shovel of earth had been thrown, they all gathered round with their plates in their hands, pushing and nudging each other with feigned animation, each reaching out for a slice of cake.

Soon the slices of cake had been distributed onto the side plates, in a silence full of commotion. The smaller children, their mouths hidden by the table and their eyes barely on a level, accompanied the distribution with mute intensity. The raisins rolled from the cake among dry crumbs. The anguished children saw the raisins scatter and their eyes attentively watched the cake gradually collapse.

And when they went up to investigate, they found the old lady already devouring her last mouthful. And the party was over, so to speak.

Cordelia was smiling and absently looking all around the room.

"I've already told you, this is no day for discussing business!" José replied, beaming.

"All right, all right then!" agreed a reconciled Emmanuel without looking at his wife, who did not take her eyes off him.

"That's all right," repeated Emmanuel, trying to smile, and a sudden contraction rapidly passed over the muscles of his face.

"This is Mother's day!" said José.

At the head of the table, the tablecloth stained with Coca-Cola and the cake reduced to crumbs, sat the mother he referred to. The old lady blinked her eyes.

There they were—fidgeting, agitated, laughing—her family. And she was mother to all of them. And if she did not suddenly rise up, as a dead man slowly rises up and strikes silence and terror in the living, the old lady stiffened in her chair and at the same time seemed taller. She was mother to all of them. And as her chain was choking her, she was mother to all of them, and, powerless in her chair, she heartily despised them. She looked at them, blinking. All those children, grandchildren, and great-grandchildren, who were nothing but the flesh of her flesh, she suddenly thought, as if she had spat. Rodrigo, her seven-year-old grandson, was the only one who could be called the flesh of her heart, Rodrigo with that stubborn little face, virile and dishevelled. Where is Rodrigo? Rodrigo with his sleepy and swollen face on that intense and bewildered little head. That one had the makings of a man. But, still blinking, the old lady studied the others. She felt such contempt for this spineless lot. What had gone wrong? How could she, who had been so strong, have been able to give birth to those weak creatures with their limp arms and anxious faces. She, the strong one, who had married at the opportune moment a good man whom, submissive yet independent, she had respected; whom she had respected and who had given her children and support and honored his obligations. The tree had been good. Yet it had rendered those bitter and unhappy fruits, without even the capacity for healthy contentment. How could she have given life to those grinning, spineless, and indulgent creatures? The rancor groaned in her empty breast. A bunch of communists, that's what they were—communists. She looked at them with senile scorn. They looked like a nest of jostling rats, and this was her family. Irrepressible, she turned her head away and, with unsuspected force, she spat on the floor.

"Mother!" called out the mortified Zilda. "What *are* you doing, Mother?" Zilda cried, stunned by shame, and she could not even bring herself to look at the others, knowing that the wretches would be looking smugly at each other as if it were her responsibility to educate the old woman, and she wouldn't put it past them to say that she no longer bathed the old woman just as they would never appreciate the sacrifice she was making on their behalf. "Mother, what *are* you doing?" she pleaded in a low voice, greatly distressed. "You have never done this sort of thing before!" she added loudly so that the others might hear, wishing to identify herself with the astonishment of everyone else—when the cock crows three times you will disown your own mother. But her extreme annoyance abated when she saw that they were shaking their heads as if in agreement that the old lady was now no more responsible than a child.

"Only recently has she started spitting," she then concluded, confiding contritely in all of them.

They all stared in silence at the old lady, full of remorse and respect.

They looked like a nest of jostling rats, and this was her family. Her sons, although grown up—probably already in their fifties, who knows!—her sons still preserved some attractive traits. But what wives they had chosen! And what wives her grandchildren—even more feeble and bitter—had chosen. All of them vain and with slender legs, with those false necklaces which break at the slightest touch, those good-for-nothing women who had made bad marriages for their children—who couldn't put a maid in her place—and all of them wearing earrings, and not one of them, not a single one made of gold! Her rage was suffocating her.

"Give me a glass of wine!" she said.

The room was struck to silence, each of them with their glass immobilized in their hand.

"Granny, won't wine do you harm?" cautiously insinuated her granddaughter, who was round and squat.

"Don't 'Granny' me!" she exploded bitterly. May the devil take you, you pack of ninnies, cuckolds, and layabouts! "Give me a glass of wine, Dorothy," she ordered.

Dorothy didn't know what to do, and with a comical expression of despair she appealed to all of them for help. But, like disembodied and unassailable masks, suddenly no face was to be seen. The interrupted party, the half-eaten sandwiches in their hands, some dry bits still in their mouths, waiting to be masticated, and puffing out their cheeks at the wrong moment.

They had all become blind, deaf, and mute, with their croquettes in their hands. And they stared impassively.

Solitary and amused, Dorothy gave her some wine, astutely pouring the smallest measure into the glass. Void of expression and prepared, they all waited for the storm.

But not only did the old lady not explode with the miserable amount of wine Dorothy had given her, but she did not even touch the glass.

Her gaze remained fixed and silent. Just as if nothing had happened.

Everyone exchanged polite glances, smiling blindly and abstractedly as if a dog had peed in the room. Stoically, the voices and laughter started up again. The daughter-in-law from Olaria, who had enjoyed her first moment of unison with the others when tragedy had triumphantly seemed about to unleash itself, was obliged to resume her solitary gloom, without even the support of her three children, who were now treacherously mixing with the others. From her cloistered chair she critically analyzed those dresses without any style, without as much as a drape and that mania they had for wearing a black dress with a string of pearls, which was worn not for fashion but economy. Examining from a distance those sandwiches that had scarcely any butter in them. She had not helped herself to a thing—not a thing! She had only accepted one of everything in order to sample them.

And, to all intents and purposes, the party had finished once more. People remained seated, looking benevolent. Some with their attention turned within themselves, waiting for something to say. Others empty and expectant with an amiable smile, their stomachs filled with all that rubbish which did not provide any nourishment yet spoiled their appetite. The children, already beyond control, were shouting their heads off. Some already had dirty faces and the tiny ones had wet diapers. The afternoon was quickly drawing to a close. And Cordelia? Cordelia looked remote, with a bewildered smile, nursing her secret to herself. "What's bothering her?" someone asked with negligent curiosity, pointing her out from afar with his head, but no one answered. They put on the rest of the lights in order to hasten the tranquillity of dusk; the children were beginning to quarrel. But the lights were more pallid than the pallid tension of the evening. And without yielding, the twilight of Copacabana meanwhile spread further and further and penetrated the windows—vast and heavy.

"I must be off," one of the daughters-in-law said anxiously, getting to her feet and shaking the crumbs from her skirt. Several people got up smiling. The old lady received a cautious kiss from each one, as if her unfamiliar skin were some kind of trap. And, blinking impassively, the old lady received those deliberately garbled words they addressed to her as they tried to give one last spurt of effusion to something that was already over: darkness had now almost completely descended. The light in the room seemed more amber and mellow, and the people in the room looked older. The children were becoming hysterical. "I wonder if she's hoping that the cake will be a substitute for dinner," the old woman pondered in her depths.

But no one could imagine what she was thinking. And for those near the door who gave her one final look, the old lady was only what she appeared to be: seated at the head of that messy table, with one hand clenched on the tablecloth as if holding a scepter, and with that silence which was her final word. With her clenched fist on the table, she would no longer be only what she thought. Her appearance had finally surpassed her and, overcoming it, she serenely grew in stature. Cordelia looked at her in terror. That fist, mute and severe on the table, was revealing something to the unhappy daughter-in-law who was helplessly loving her perhaps for the last time. "One must know. One must know. Life is so short. Life is so short."

However, the sign was not repeated. Because truth came in

a glance. Cordelia looked at her in utter dismay. And no more, not even once more was the sign repeated, while Rodrigo, the old lady's grandson, tugged the hand of that guilty mother, perplexed and desperate, who once more looked back imploring from old age one more sign that a woman must, in one lacerating impulse, finally hold on to her last chance to live. Just once more Cordelia sought to look. But when she looked this time the honoree of the day was merely an old woman at the head of the table.

The sudden sign had passed. And, tugged by the impatient and insistent hand of Rodrigo, her daughter-in-law followed him in terror.

"Not everyone has the privilege and the honor of being reunited with their mother on her birthday," José croaked, remembering that it was Jonga who used to make the speeches.

"With their mother, period!" quietly laughed his niece, and her cousin, who was slow on the uptake, laughed without being amused.

"We have," said a downcast Emmanuel, without daring to glance further at his wife, "we have this great privilege," he said in distraction as he dried the sweat from the palms of his hands.

But it was nothing of the sort, only the uneasiness of departure, never really knowing what to say, José waiting with perseverence and confidence for the next sentence of the speech to come out. Which failed to come. Which did not come. Which did not come. The others waited. How he missed Jonga at moments like this—José wiped his forehead with his handkerchief—how he missed Jonga at moments like this!

Also, Jonga had been the only member of the family of whom the old woman had approved, and respected, and this had given Jonga so much confidence. And when he had died, the old woman had never more mentioned his name, placing a barrier between his death and the others. Perhaps she had forgotten him. But she had not forgotten that same steady and direct gaze with which she had always looked at her other children, forcing them to look away. A mother's love was difficult to bear. José wiped his forehead, heroic and smiling.

And suddenly the phrase came.

"How about next year!" José suddenly exclaimed with a hint of malice unexpectedly finding the right phrase: a nice touch of innuendo! "How about next year, hm?" he repeated, afraid of not having been understood.

He looked at her, proud of the cunning of the old woman, who always slyly managed to live for another year.

"Next year we'll be back in front of the birthday cake with its lighted candle!" specified her son Emanuel, improving on his partner's wit. "How about next year, Mother! In front of the birthday cake!" he carefully pronounced into her ear, while he looked obsequiously at José. And the old woman suddenly cackled with a feeble smile upon grasping the allusion.

Then she opened her mouth and said, "That's right."

Encouraged by the fact that everything had turned out so surprisingly well, José called to her, moved and grateful, with moist eyes, "We'll see each other next year, Mother."

"I'm not deaf!" the old woman retorted brusquely, reacting to their endearments.

Her sons looked at each other, smiling, annoyed, and happy. Everything had turned out perfectly.

The children left in high spirits with their appetites ruined. The daughter-in-law from Olaria gave a vindictive slap to her son who was behaving wildly and had shed his tie. The stairs were awkward and dark; how incredible that anyone should insist on living in that squalid building which would be demolished any day now, and, once they were evicted, Zilda would be ready to give more trouble and would want to push the old girl onto the daughters-in-law. Reaching the bottom of the stairs with some relief, the guests found themselves in the cool tranquillity of the street. It was certainly evening. With its first hints of cold.

"So long, we must keep in touch." "Come and see us," they said rapidly. Some managed to look into the eyes of others with a friendliness free of distrust. Others buttoned up their children's coats, looking at the sky for some indication of the weather. All of them feeling obscurely that in their farewell one could perhaps, now without any danger of compromise, be good and say that extra word—but what word? They didn't quite know and they looked at each other, smiling—and silent. It was a moment which was seeking to come alive. But which was dead. They began to break up, turning away, without knowing how to take leave of their relatives without being abrupt.

"How about next year!" José repeated his felicitous remark, waving his hand with effusive vigor, his sparse white hair blowing about. "How fat he was getting," they thought, "and he ought to be taking care with that heart of his." "How about next year!" called José, eloquent and large, and his tall frame looked as if it might collapse. But the persons who had moved away did not know whether they should laugh aloud so that he could hear them or if it were sufficient to smile quietly in the dark. Furthermore, some of them thought that happily there was more than a joke to his innuendo and that not until the following year would they be obliged to meet each other again, in front of the birthday cake; while others, already hidden in the darkness of the street, wondered if the old woman would be able to withstand Zilda's neurosis and impatience for another year; not that they could really be expected to do anything about it. "At least ninety years," sadly thought the daughter-in-law from Ipanema. "In order to reach a nice ripe age," she thought dreamily.

Meantime, up there, above stairs and contingencies, the old

lady who was celebrating her birthday sat at the head of the table, erect and definitive, larger than life. "Perhaps we shall not be having any dinner tonight," she mused. Death was her mystery.

The Smallest Woman in the World

In the depths of equatorial Africa the French explorer, Marcel Pretre, hunter and man of the world, came across a tribe of pygmies of surprising minuteness. He was even more surprised, however, to learn that an even smaller race existed far beyond the forests. So he traveled more deeply into the jungle.

In the Central Congo he discovered, in fact, the smallest pygmies in the world. And—like a box inside another box, inside yet another box—among the smallest pygmies in the world, he found the smallest of the smallest pygmies in the world, answering, perhaps, to the need that Nature sometimes feels to surpass herself.

Among the mosquitoes and the trees moist with humidity, among the luxuriant vegetation of the most indolent green, Marcel Pretre came face to face with a woman no more than forty-five centimeters tall, mature, black, and silent. "As black as a monkey," he would inform the newspapers, and she lived at the top of a tree with her little mate. In the warm humidity of the forest, which matured the fruits quickly and gave them an unbearably sweet taste, she was pregnant. Meanwhile there she stood, the smallest woman in the world. For a second, in the drone of the jungle heat, it was as if the Frenchman had unexpectedly arrived at the end of the line. Certainly, it was only because he was sane that he managed to keep his head and not lose control. Sensing a sudden need to restore order, and to give a name to what exists, he called her Little Flower. And, in order to be able to classify her among the identifiable realities, he immediately began to gather data about her.

Her race is slowly being exterminated. Few human examples remain of their species which, were it not for the subtle dangers of Africa, would be a widely scattered race.

Excluding disease, the polluted air of its rivers, deficiencies of food, and wild beasts on the prowl, the greatest hazard for the few remaining Likoualas are the savage Bantus, a threat which surrounds them in the silent air as on the morning of battle. The Bantus pursue them with nets as they pursue monkeys. And they eat them. Just like that: they pursue them with nets and eat them. So this race of tiny people went on retreating and retreating until it finally settled in the heart of Africa where the fortunate explorer was to discover them. As a strategic defense, they live in the highest trees. The women come down in order to cook maize, grind mandioca, and gather green vegetables; the men to hunt. When a child is born, he is given his freedom almost at once. Often, one must concede, the child does not enjoy his freedom for long among the wild beasts of the jungle, but, at least, he cannot complain that for such a short life the labor had been long. Even the language that the child learns is short and simple, consisting only of the essentials. The Likoualas use few names and they refer to things by gestures and animal noises. As a spiritual enhancement, he possesses his drum. While they dance to the sound of the drum, a tiny male keeps watch for the Bantus, who appear from heaven knows where.

This, then, was how the explorer discovered at his feet the smallest human creature that exists. His heart pounded, for surely no emerald is so rare. Not even the teachings of the Indian sages are so rare, and even the richest man in the world has not witnessed such strange charm. There, before his eyes, stood a woman such as the delights of the most exquisite dream had never equaled. It was then that the explorer timidly pronounced with a delicacy of feeling of which even his wife would never have believed him capable, "You are Little Flower."

At that moment, Little Flower scratched herself where one never scratches oneself. The explorer—as if he were receiving the highest prize of chastity to which man, always so full of ideals, dare aspire—the explorer who has so much experience of life, turned away his eyes.

The photograph of Little Flower was published in the color supplement of the Sunday newspapers, where she was reproduced life size. She appeared wrapped in a shawl, with her belly in an advanced stage. Her nose was flat, her face black, her eyes deep-set, and her feet splayed. She looked just like a dog.

That same Sunday, in an apartment, a woman, glancing at the picture of Little Flower in the open newspaper, did not care to look a second time, "because it distresses me."

In another apartment, a woman felt such a perverse tenderness for the daintiness of the African woman that—prevention being better than cure—Little Flower should never be left alone with the tenderness of that woman. Who knows to what darkness of love her affection might extend. The woman passed a troubled day, overcome, one might say, by desire. Besides, it was spring and there was a dangerous longing in the air.

In another house, a little five-year-old girl, upon seeing Little Flower's picture and listening to the comments of her parents, became frightened. In that house of adults, this little girl had been, until now, the smallest of human beings. And, if this was the source of the nicest endearments, it was also the source of that first fear of tyrannical love. The existence of Little Flower caused the little girl to feel—with a vagueness which only many years later, and, for quite different reasons, she was to experience as a concrete thought—caused her to feel with premature awareness, that "misfortune knows no limits."

In another house, in the consecration of spring, a young girl about to be married burst out compassionately, "Mother, look at her picture, poor little thing! Just look at her sad expression!"

"Yes," replied the girl's mother—hard, defeated, and proud —"but that is the sadness of an animal, not of a human."

"Oh Mother!" the girl protested in despair.

It was in another house that a bright child had a bright idea.

"Mummy, what if I were to put this tiny woman in little Paul's bed while he is sleeping? When he wakes up, what a fright he'll get, eh? What a din he'll make when he finds her sitting up in bed beside him! And then we could play with her! We could make her our toy, eh!"

His mother, at that moment, was rolling her hair in front of the bathroom mirror, and she remembered what the cook had told her about her time as an orphan. Not having any dolls to play with, and maternal feelings already stirring furiously in their hearts, some deceitful girls in the orphanage had concealed from the nun in charge the death of one of their companions. They kept her body in a cupboard until Sister went out, and then they played with the dead girl, bathing her and feeding her little tidbits, and they punished her only to be able to kiss and comfort her afterward.

The mother recalled this in the bathroom and she lowered her awkward hands, full of hairpins. And she considered the cruel necessity of loving. She considered the malignity of our desire to be happy. She considered the ferocity with which we want to play. And the number of times when we murder for love. She then looked at her mischievous son as if she were looking at a dangerous stranger. And she was horrified at her own soul, which, more than her body, had engendered that being so apt for life and happiness. And thus she looked at him, attentively and with uneasy pride, her child already without two front teeth, his evolution, his evolution under way, his teeth falling out to make room for those which bite best. "I must buy him a new suit," she decided, looking at him intently. She obstinately dressed up her toothless child in fancy clothes, and obstinately insisted upon keeping him clean and tidy, as if cleanliness might give emphasis to a tranquilizing superficiality, obstinately perfecting the polite aspect of beauty. Obstinately removing herself, and removing him from something which must be as "black as a monkey." Then, looking into the bathroom mirror, the mother smiled, intentionally refined and polished, placing between that face of hers of abstract lines and the raw face of Little Flower, the insuperable distance of millenia. But with years of experience she knew that this would be a Sunday on which she would have to conceal from herself her anxiety, her dream, and the lost millenia.

In another house, against a wall, they set about the exciting business of calculating with a measuring tape the forty-five centimeters of Little Flower. And as they enjoyed themselves they made a startling discovery: she was even smaller than the most penetrating imagination could ever have invented. In the heart of each member of the family there arose the gnawing desire to possess that minute and indomitable thing for himself, that thing which had been saved from being devoured, that enduring fount of charity. The eager soul of that family was roused to dedication. And, indeed, who has not wanted to possess a human being just for himself? A thing, it is true, which would not always be convenient, for there are moments when one would choose not to have sentiments.

"I'll bet you if she lived here we would finish up quarreling," said the father, seated in his armchair, firmly turning the pages of the newspaper. "In this house everything finishes up with a quarrel."

"You are always such a pessimist, José," said the mother.

"Mother, can you imagine how tiny her little child will be?" their oldest girl, thirteen, asked intensely.

The father fidgeted behind his newspaper.

"It must be the smallest black baby in the world," replied the mother, melting with pleasure. "Just imagine her waiting on table here in the house! And with her swollen little belly."

"That's enough of that rubbish!" muttered the father, annoyed.

"You must admit," said the mother, unexpectedly peeved, "that the thing is unique. You are the one who is insensitive."

And what about the unique thing itself?

Meanwhile, in Africa, the unique thing itself felt in its heart —perhaps also black, because one can no longer have confidence in a Nature that had already blundered once—meanwhile the unique thing itself felt in its heart something still more rare, rather like the secret of its own secret: a minute child. Methodically, the explorer examined with his gaze the belly of the smallest mature human being. It was at that moment that the explorer, for the first time since he had known her—instead of experiencing curiosity, enthusiasm, a sense of triumph, or the excitement of discovery—felt distinctly ill at ease.

The fact is that the smallest woman in the world was smiling. She was smiling and warm, warm. Little Flower was enjoying herself. The unique thing itself was enjoying the ineffable sen-

sation of not having been devoured yet. Not to have been devoured was something which at other times gave her the sudden impulse to leap from branch to branch. But at this tranquil
moment, among the dense undergrowth of the Central Congo,
she was not applying that impulse to an action—and the impulse concentrated itself completely in the very smallness of the
unique thing itself. And suddenly she was smiling. It was a
smile that only someone who does not speak can smile. A smile
that the uncomfortable explorer did not succeed in classifying.
And she went on enjoying her own gentle smile, she who was
not being devoured. Not to be devoured is the most perfect
sentiment. Not to be devoured is the secret objective of a whole
existence. While she was not being devoured, her animal smile
was as delicate as happiness. The explorer felt disconcerted.

In the second place, if the unique thing itself was smiling it
was because, inside her minute body, a great darkness had
started to stir.

It is that the unique thing itself felt her breast warm with
that which might be called love. She loved that yellow explorer.
If she knew how to speak and should say that she loved him, he
would swell with pride. Pride that would diminish when she
should add that she also adored the explorer's ring and his
boots. And when he became deflated with disappointment,
Little Flower would fail to understand. Because, not even remotely, would her love for the explorer—one can even say her
"deep love," because without other resources she was reduced
to depth—since not even remotely would her deep love for the
explorer lose its value because she also loved his boots. There
is an old misunderstanding about the word "love," and if many
children are born on account of that mistake, many others have
lost the unique instant of birth simply on account of a suscepti-
bility which exacts that it should be me, me that should be
loved and not my money. But in the humidity of the jungle,
there do not exist these cruel refinements; love is not to be de-

voured, love is to find boots pretty, love is to like the strange color of a man who is not black, love is to smile out of love at a ring that shines. Little Flower blinked with love and smiled, warm, small, pregnant, and warm.

The explorer tried to smile back at her, without knowing exactly to which charm his smile was replying, and then became disturbed as only a full-grown man becomes disturbed. He tried to conceal his uneasiness, by adjusting his helmet on his head, and he blushed with embarrassment. He turned a pretty color, his own, greenish pink hue, like that of a lime in the morning light. He must be sour.

It was probably upon adjusting his symbolic helmet that the explorer called himself to order, returned severely to the discipline of work, and resumed taking notes. He had learned to understand some of the few words articulated by the tribe and to interpret their signs. He was already able to ask questions.

Little Flower answered "yes." That it was very nice to have a tree in which to live by herself, all by herself. Because—and this she did not say, but her eyes became so dark that they said it—because it is nice to possess, so nice to possess. The explorer blinked several times.

Marcel Pretre experienced a few difficult moments trying to control himself. But at least he was kept occupied in taking notes. Anyone not taking notes had to get along as best he could.

"Well, it just goes to show," an old woman suddenly exclaimed, folding her newspaper with determination, "it just goes to show. I'll say one thing though—God knows what He's about."

The Dinner

He came into the restaurant late. No doubt he had been detained until then over important business. His appearance suggested a man in his sixties, tall, corpulent, with grey hair, bushy eyebrows, and powerful hands. On one finger the ring symbolizing his power. He sat down, broad and solid.

I lost sight of him, and, as I ate, I glanced once more at the thin woman in a large hat. She was laughing with her mouth full and her dark eyes sparkled.

Just as I was lifting the fork to my mouth, I saw him. There he sat with his eyes shut, mechanically chewing his bread with obvious pleasure, both his fists clenched on the table. I went on eating and watching him. The waiter set out the plates on the table cloth, but the elderly gentleman remained with his eyes closed. As the waiter made some livelier gesture, he opened his eyes so abruptly that their movement simultaneously communicated with his enormous hands and a fork dropped on the floor. The waiter murmured words of reassurance as he bent down to retrieve it, but the man offered no comment. Now fully awake, he was suddenly turning his meat from one side to another, examining it vehemently, the tip of his tongue showing, prodding the steak with the back of his fork, almost sniffing at it, his mouth already in action. And he began to cut the meat with a vigorous movement which involved his whole body and seemed quite superfluous. After a short pause, he lifted a piece of meat to a certain height, level with his face, and, as if required to catch it in flight, he snatched it with one swift movement of his head. I looked down at my plate. When I looked up again, he was completely absorbed in enjoying his dinner, chewing with open mouth and licking his teeth with his tongue, his gaze fixed on the ceiling light. I was about to cut myself another piece of meat when I saw him come to a complete halt.

And as if he could bear it no longer—but what?—he quickly grabbed his napkin and dabbed round his eyes with his hairy hands. I stopped to watch. His body breathed with difficulty and appeared to swell. Finally, he lowered his napkin from his face and stared numbly into space. He panted, opening and closing his eyelids in a startling manner, and, carefully wiping his eyes, he slowly chewed the rest of the food still in his mouth.

A second later, however, he seemed revived and once more impenetrable: he seized a forkful of salad with his entire frame and ate with his head leaning forward, the line of his jaw giving an impression of disdain, the oil moistening his lips. He then paused for a moment, dried his eyes again, briefly swung his head—and another forkful of lettuce and meat was caught in mid-air.

He called to the passing waiter, "This is not the wine I ordered."

Exactly the tone of voice I would have expected of him: a voice that invited no rejoinder, and I saw that no one could ever do anything for him. Except obey.

The waiter courteously withdrew, carrying the bottle. But suddenly the elderly gentleman stiffened once more as if his chest were constricted by some obstruction. His mighty strength was suddenly frustrated. He waited . . . until the hunger seemed to assault him and he began to chew heartily again, his eyebrows furrowed in a frown. I had already started to eat slowly, slightly nauseated without knowing why, taking part in something I could not understand. Suddenly he started to shake from head to foot, raised his napkin to his eyes and pressed them with a brutality which enthralled me. With a certain decisiveness, I put my fork down on my plate, as I, too, experienced an unbearable choking in my throat, and I felt furious and forced into submission. But the elderly gentleman did not pause for long, holding his napkin to his eyes. This time, when he unhurriedly removed it, his pupils were extremely relaxed and tired, and before he could dry them—I saw something. I saw a tear.

I leaned over my meat, lost. When I finally managed to confront him from the depths of my pallid face, I observed that he, too, was leaning forward, his elbows resting on the table, his head between his hands. And obviously he could bear it no longer. His bushy eyebrows were touching. His food must have lodged just below his throat under the stress of his emotion, for when he was able to continue, he made a visible effort to swallow, dabbing his forehead with his napkin. I could bear it no longer, the meat on my plate was raw . . . and I really could not bear it another minute. But he—he was eating.

The waiter brought a bottle in a bucket of ice. I noted every detail without being capable of discrimination. The bottle was different, the waiter in tails, and the light haloed the robust head of Pluto which was now moving with curiosity, greedy and attentive. For a second the waiter obliterated my view of the elderly gentleman and I could only see his black coattails hovering over the table as he poured red wine into the glass and waited with ardent eyes—because here was surely a man who would tip generously, one of those elderly gentlemen who still command attention . . . and power. The elderly gentleman, who now seemed larger, confidently took a sip, lowered his glass, and sourly considered the taste in his mouth. He compressed his lips and smacked them with distaste, as if the good were also intolerable. I waited, the waiter waited, and we both leaned forward in suspense. Finally he made a grimace of approval. The waiter curved his shiny head in submission to the man's words of thanks and went off with lowered head, while I sighed with relief.

He now mingled gulps of wine with the meat in his great mouth and his false teeth ponderously chewed while I observed him . . . in vain. Nothing more happened. The restaurant appeared to radiate with renewed intensity under the tinkling of glass and cutlery; in the brightly lit dome of the room the whispered conversations rose and fell in gentle waves; the woman in the large hat smiled with half-closed eyes, looking slender and beautiful as the waiter carefully poured the wine into her glass. But now he was making another gesture.

With a ponderous hairy hand, in the palm of which destiny had drawn such lines, he made a pensive gesture; it expressed, in mime, as much as it could, yet alas I failed to understand. And, as if he could no longer go on, he put down his fork on his plate. This time you let yourself be caught, old man. He sat there breathing heavily and visibly weary. He then held his glass of wine and drank with his eyes closed, in sonorous resurrection. My eyes were burning and the brightness was intense and persistent. I felt gripped by the heaving ecstasy of nausea.

Everything seemed to loom large and dangerous. The slender woman, appearing ever more beautiful, shivered gravely among the lights.

He finished eating, his face drained of expression. He shut his eyes and distended his jaws. I tried to take advantage of this moment in which he no longer had his own face, in order to discover something at last. But it was useless. The great apparition before me meant nothing to me . . . regal, cruel and blind. What I wanted to confront directly, on account of the extraordinary strength of the elderly gentleman, ceased to exist at that moment. He refused to yield.

The dessert arrived, a melted cream, and I registered surprise at the decadence of his choice. He ate slowly, lifted a spoonful to his mouth and watched the creamy liquid trickle. He swallowed the lot, despite making a grimace and, now grown and nourished, he pushed away his plate. No longer hungry, the great horse rested his head on one hand. The first clear sign began to appear. The old child-eater was deep in meditation. With a pale expression I saw him raise his napkin to his mouth. I imagined that I could hear him sobbing, but we both kept silent in the center of the room. Perhaps he had eaten too quickly. Because, despite everything, you hadn't lost your hunger, eh? I provoked him with irony, rage, and exhaustion. But he was visibly collapsing. His expression was now crestfallen and imbecilic, and he was swaying his head from one side to another—from one side to the other, unable to control himself any longer, his mouth tightly drawn, his eyes shut as he swayed to and fro—the patriarch was crying to himself.

Rage choked me. I saw him put on his spectacles and become much older. As he counted his change, his teeth pushed his chin forward, surrendering for a moment to the kindness of old age. Even I, so intently was I studying him, did not notice him take out his money to pay, nor see him examine the bill, nor the waiter return with the change.

Finally he removed his spectacles, clicked his teeth and dried his eyes, making futile and painful grimaces. He passed his broad hand through his grey hair, smoothing it down with authority. Then he stood up, steadying himself on the edge of the table with his vigorous hands. And there, suddenly deprived of any support, he seemed less mighty, although still enormous and capable of stabbing any one of us present. Powerless to act, I watched him putting on his hat and adjusting his tie in the mirror. He then crossed the brightness of the room and disappeared.

But I am still a man.

When I have been betrayed and slaughtered, when someone has gone away forever, or I have lost the best of my possessions, or when I have learned that I am about to die—I do not eat. I have not yet attained this power, this edifice, this ruin. I push away my plate, I reject the meat and its blood.

Preciousness

Early in the morning it was always the same thing renewed: to awaken. A thing that was slow, extended, vast. Vastly, she opened her eyes.

She was fifteen years old and she was not pretty. But inside her thinness existed the almost majestic vastness in which she stirred, as in a meditation. And within the mist there was something precious. Which did not extend itself, did not compromise itself nor contaminate itself. Which was intense like a jewel. Herself.

She awakened before the others, since to go to school she would have to catch a bus and a train and this would take her an hour. This would also give her an hour. Of daydreams as acute as a crime. The morning breeze violating the window and her face until her lips became hard and icy cold. Then she was smiling. As if smiling in itself were an objective. All this would happen if she were fortunate enough to "avoid having anyone look at her."

When she got up in the morning—the moment of vastness having passed in which everything unfolded—she hastily dressed, persuaded herself that she had no time to take a bath, and her family, still asleep, would never guess how few she took. Under the burning lamp in the dining room she swallowed her coffee which the maid, scratching herself in the gloom of the kitchen, had reheated. She scarcely touched the bread which the butter failed to soften. With her mouth fresh from fasting, her books under her arm, she finally opened the door and passed quickly from the stale warmth of the house into the cold fruition of the morning. Where she no longer felt any need to hurry. She has to cross a long deserted road before reaching the avenue, from the end of which a bus would emerge swaying in the morning haze, with its headlights still lit. In the June breeze, the mysterious act, authoritarian and perfect, was to raise one's arm—and already from afar the trembling bus began to become distorted, obeying the arrogance of her body, representative of a supreme power; from afar the bus started to become uncertain and slow, slow and advancing, every moment more concrete—until it pulled up before her, belching heat and smoke, smoke and heat. Then she got on, as serious as a missionary, because of the workers on the bus who "might say something to her." Those men who were no longer just boys. But she was also afraid of boys, and afraid of the youngest ones too. Afraid they would "say something to her," would look her up and down. In the seriousness of her closed lips there was a great plea: that they should respect her. More than this. As if she had made some vow, she was obliged to be venerated and while, deep inside, her heart beat with fear, she too venerated herself, she, the custodian of a rhythm. If they watched her, she became rigid and sad.

What spared her was that men did not notice her. Although something inside her, as her sixteen years gradually approached in heat and smoke—something might be intensely surprised—and this might surprise some men. As if someone had touched her on the shoulder. A shadow perhaps. On the ground the enormous shadow of a girl without a man, an uncertain element capable of being crystallized which formed part of the monotonous geometry of the great public ceremonies. As if they had touched her on the shoulder. They watched her yet did not see her. She cast a greater shadow than the reality that existed. In the bus the workmen were silent with their lunch boxes on their laps, sleep still hovering on their faces. She felt ashamed at not trusting them, tired as they were. But until she could forget them, she felt uneasy. The fact is that they "knew." And since she knew too, hence her disquiet. Her father also knew. An old man begging alms knew. Wealth distributed, and silence.

Later, with the gait of a soldier, she crossed—unscathed—the Largo da Lapa, where day had broken. At this point the battle was almost won. On the tram she chose an empty seat, if at all possible, or, if she was lucky, she sat down beside some reassuring woman with a bundle of clothes on her lap, for example—and that was the first truce. Once at school, she would still have to confront the long corridor where her fellow pupils would be standing in conversation, and where the heels of her shoes made a noise that her tense legs were unable to suppress as if she were vainly trying to silence the beating of a heart—those shoes with their own dance rhythm. A vague silence emerged among the boys who perhaps sensed, beneath her pretense, that she was one of the prudes. She passed between the aisles of her fellow pupils growing in stature, and they did not know what to think or say. The noise made by her shoes was ugly. She gave away her own secret with her wooden heels.

If the corridor should last a little longer, as if she had forgotten her destiny, she would run with her hands over her ears. She only possessed sturdy shoes. As if they were still the same ones they had solemnly put on her at birth. She crossed the corridor, which seemed as interminable as the silence in a trench and in her expression there was something so ferocious—and proud too because of her shadow—that no one said a word to her. Prohibitive, she forbade them to think.

Until at last she reached the classroom. Where suddenly everything became unimportant and more rapid and light, where her face revealed some freckles, her hair fell over her eyes, and where she was treated like a boy. Where she was intelligent. The astute profession. She appeared to have studied at home. Her curiosity instructed her more than the answers she was given. She divined—feeling in her mouth the bitter taste of heroic pains—she divined the fascinated repulsion her thinking head created in her companions who, once more, did not know what to say about her. Each time more, the great deceiver became more intelligent. She had learned to think. The necessary sacrifice: in this way "no one dared."

At times, while the teacher was speaking, she, intense, nebulous, drew symmetrical lines on her exercise book. If a line, which had to be at the same time both strong and delicate, went outside the imaginary circle where it belonged, everything would collapse: she became self-absorbed and remote, guided by the avidity of her ideal. Sometimes, instead of lines, she drew stars, stars, stars, so many and so high that she came out of this task of foretelling exhausted, lifting her drowsy head.

The return journey home was so full of hunger that impatience and hatred gnawed at her heart. Returning home it seemed another city: in the Largo da Lapa hundreds of people reflected by her hunger seemed to have forgotten, and if they remembered they would bare their teeth. The sun outlined each man with black charcoal. Her own shadow was a black post.

At this hour, in which greater caution had to be exercised, she was protected by the kind of ugliness which her hunger accentuated, her features darkened by the adrenaline that darkened the flesh of animals of prey. In the empty house, with the whole family out and about their business, she shouted at the maid who did not even answer. She ate like a centaur. Her face close to her plate, her hair almost in her food.

"Skinny, but you can eat all right," the quick-witted maid was saying.

"Go to blazes," she shouted at her sullenly.

In the empty house, alone with the maid, she no longer walked like a soldier, she no longer needed to exercise caution. But she missed the battle of the streets: the melancholy of freedom, with the horizon still so very remote. She had surrendered to the horizon. But the nostalgia of the present. The lesson of patience, the vow to wait. From which perhaps she might never know how to free herself. The afternoon transforming itself into something interminable and until they all might return home to dinner and she might become to her relief a daughter, there was this heat, her book opened and then closed, an intuition, this heat: she sat down with her head between her hands, feeling desperate. When she was ten, she remembered, a little boy who loved her had thrown a dead rat at her. "Dirty thing!" she had screamed, white with indignation. It had been an experience. She had never told anyone. With her head between her hands, seated. She said fifteen times, "I am well, I am well, I am well," then she realized that she had barely paid attention to the score. Adding to the total, she said once more: "I am well, sixteen." And now she was no longer at the mercy of anyone. Desperate because well and free, she was no longer at anyone's mercy. She had lost her faith. She went to converse with the maid, the ancient priestess. They recognized each other. The two of them barefooted in the kitchen, the smoke rising from the stove. She had lost her faith, but on the border of grace, she sought in the maid only what the latter had already lost, not what she had gained. She pretended to be distracted and, conversing, she avoided conversation. "She imagines that at my age I must know more than I do, in fact, and she is capable of teaching me something," she thought, her head between her hands, defending her ignorance with her body. There were elements missing, but she did not want them from someone who had already forgotten them. The great wait was part of it. And inside that vastness—scheming.

All this, certainly. Prolonged, exhausted, the exasperation. But on the following morning, as an ostrich slowly uncurls its head, she awoke. She awoke to the same intact mystery, and opening her eyes she was the princess of that intact mystery.

As if the factory horn had already whistled, she dressed hastily and downed her coffee in one gulp. She opened the front door. And then she no longer hurried. The great immolation of the streets. Sly, alert, the wife of an apache. A part of the primitive rhythm of a ritual.

It was an even colder and darker morning than the previous ones, and she shivered in her sweater. The white mist left the end of the road invisible. Everything seemed to be enveloped in cotton-wool, one could not even hear the noise of the buses passing along the avenue. She went on walking along the uncertain path of the road. The houses slept behind closed doors. The gardens were hard with frost. In the dark air, not in the sky, but in the middle of the road, there was a star: a great star of ice which had not yet disappeared, hovering uncertainly in the air, humid and formless. Surprised in its delay, it grew round in its hesitation. She looked at the nearby star. She walked alone in the bombarded city.

No, she was not alone. Her eyes glowering with disbelief, at the far end of her street, within the mist, she spied two men. Two youths coming toward her. She looked around her as if she might have mistaken the road or the city. But she had mistaken the minutes; she had left the house before the star and the two men had time to disappear. Her heart contracted with fear.

Her first impulse, confronted with her error, was to retrace her steps and go back into the house until they had passed. "They are going to look at me, I know, there is no one else for them to stare at and they are going to stare at me!" But how could she turn back and escape, if she had been born for difficulties. If her entire slow preparation was to have the unknown outcome to which she, through her devotion, had to adhere, how could she retreat, and then never more forget the shame of having waited in misery behind a door?

And perhaps there might not even be danger. They would not have the courage to say anything because she would pass with a firm gait, her mouth set, moving in her Spanish rhythm.

On heroic legs, she went on walking. As she approached, they also approached—and then they all approached and the road became shorter and shorter. The shoes of the two youths mingled with the noise of her own shoes and it was awful to listen to. It was insistent to listen to. Either their shoes were hollow or the ground was hollow. The stones on the ground gave warning. Everything was hollow and she was listening, powerless to prevent it, the silence of the enclosure communicating with the other streets in the district, and she saw, powerless to prevent it, that the doors had become more securely locked. Even the star had disappeared. In the new pallor of darkness, the road surrendered to the three of them. She was walking and listening to the men, since she could not see them and since she had to know them. She could hear them and surprised herself with her own courage. It was the gift. And the great vocation for a destiny. She advanced, suffering as she obeyed. If she could succeed in thinking about something else, she would not hear their shoes. Nor what they might be saying. Nor the silence in which their paths would cross.

With brusque rigidity she looked at them. When she least expected it, carrying the vow of secrecy, she saw them rapidly. Were they smiling? No, they were serious.

She should not have seen. Because, by seeing, she for an instant was in danger of becoming an individual, and they also. That was what she seemed to have been warned about: so long as she could preserve a world of classical harmony, so long as she remained impersonal, she would be the daughter of the gods, and assisted by that which must be accomplished. But, having seen that which eyes, upon seeing, diminish, she had put herself in danger of being "herself"—a thing tradition did not protect.

For an instant she hesitated completely, lost for a direction to take. But it was too late to retreat. It would not be too late only if she ran; but to run would mean going completely astray, and losing the rhythm that still sustained her, the rhythm that was her only talisman—given to her on the edge of the world where it was for her being alone—on the edge of the world where all memories had been obliterated, and as an incomprehensible reminder, the blind talisman had remained as the rhythm for her destiny to copy, executing it for the consummation of the whole world. Not her own. If she were to run, that order would be altered. And she would never be pardoned her greatest error: haste. And even when one escapes they run behind one, these are things one knows.

Rigid, like a catechist, without altering for a second the slowness with which she advanced, she continued to advance.

"They are going to look at me, I know!" But she tried, through the instinct of a previous life, not to betray her fear. She divined what fear was unleashing. It was to be rapid and painless. Only for a fraction of a second would their paths cross, rapid, instantaneous, because of the advantage in her favor of her being in movement and of them coming in the opposite direction, which would allow the instant to be reduced to the necessary essential

—to the collapse of the first of the seven mysteries so secret that only one knowledge of them remained: the number seven.

"Don't let them say anything, only let them think, I don't mind them thinking."

It would be rapid, and a second after the encounter she would say, in astonishment, striding through other and yet other streets, "It almost didn't hurt." But what in fact followed had no explanation.

What followed were four awkward hands, four awkward hands that did not know what they wanted, four mistaken hands of someone without a vocation, four hands that touched her so unexpectedly that she did the best thing that she could have done in the world of movement: she became paralyzed. They, whose premeditated part was merely that of passing alongside the darkness of her fear, and then the first of the seven mysteries would collapse; they, who would represent but the horizon of a single approaching step, had failed to understand their function and, with the individuality of those who experience fear, they had attacked. It had lasted less than a fraction of a second in that tranquil street. Within a fraction of a second, they touched her as if all seven mysteries belonged to them. Which she preserved in their entirety and became the more a larva and felt seven more years behind.

She did not look at them because her face was turned with serenity toward the void.

But on account of the haste with which they wounded her, she realized that they were more frightened than she was. So terrified that they were no longer there. They were running.

"They were afraid that she might call out for help and that the doors of the houses might open one by one," she reasoned. They did not know that one does not call out for help.

She remained standing, listening in a tranquil frenzy to the sound of their shoes in flight. The pavement was hollow or their shoes were hollow or she herself was hollow. In the hollow sound of their shoes she listened attentively to the fear of both youths. The sound beat clearly on the paving stones as if they were beating incessantly on a door and she were waiting for them to stop. So clear on the bareness of the stone that the tapping of their steps did not seem to grow any more distant: it was there at her feet like a dance of victory. Standing, she had nowhere to sustain herself unless by her hearing.

The sonority did not diminish, their departure was transmitted to her by a scurry of heels ever more precise. Those heels no longer echoed on the pavement, they resounded in the air like castanets, becoming ever more delicate. Then she perceived that for some time now she had heard no further sound. And, carried back by the wind, the silence and an empty road.

Until this moment, she had kept quiet, standing in the middle of the pavement. Then, as if there were several phases of the same immobility, she remained still. A moment later she sighed. And in a new phase she kept still.

She then slowly retreated back toward a wall, hunched up, moving very slowly, as if she had a broken arm, until she was leaning against the wall, where she remained inscribed. And there she remained quite still.

"Not to move is what matters," she thought from afar, "not to move." After a time, she would probably have said to herself, "Now, move your legs a little, very slowly," after which, she sighed and remained quiet, watching. It was still dark.

Then the day broke. Slowly she retrieved her books scattered on the ground. Further ahead lay her open exercise book. When she bent over to pick it up, she saw the large round handwriting which until this morning had been hers.

Then she left. Without knowing how she had filled in the time, unless with steps and more steps, she arrived at the school more than two hours late. Since she had thought about nothing, she did not realize how the time had slipped by. From the presence of the Latin master she discovered with polite surprise that in class they had already started on the third hour.

"What happened to you?" whispered the girl with the satchel at her side.

"Why?"

"Your face is white. Are you feeling unwell?"

"No," she said so clearly that several pupils looked at her. She got up and said in a loud voice, "Excuse me!"

She went to the lavatory. Where, before the great silence of the tiles, she cried out in a high shrill voice, "I am all alone in the world! No one will ever help me, no one will ever love me! I am all alone in the world!"

She was standing there, also missing the third class, on the long lavatory bench in front of several wash basins.

"It doesn't matter, I'll copy the notes later, I'll borrow some-one's notes and copy them later at home—I am all alone in the world!"

She interrupted herself, beating her clenched fists several times on the bench.

The noise of four shoes suddenly began like a fine and rapid downpour of rain. A blind noise, nothing was reflected on the shiny bricks. Only the clearness of each shoe which never be-came entangled even once with another shoe. Like nuts falling. It was only a question of waiting as one waits for them to stop knocking on the door. Then they stopped.

When she went to set her hair in front of the mirror, she looked so ugly.

She possessed so little, and they had touched her.

She was so ugly and precious.

Her face was pale, her features grown refined. Her hands, still stained with ink from the previous day, moistening her hair.

"I must take more care of myself," she thought. She did not know how to. The truth is that each time she knew even less how to. The expression of her nose was that of a snout peeping through a hedge.

She went back to the bench and sat down quietly, with her snout.

"A person is nothing. No," she retorted in weak protest, "don't say that," she thought with kindness and melancholy. "A person is something," she said in kindness.

But, during dinner, life assumed an urgent and hysterical meaning.

"I need some new shoes! Mine make a lot of noise, a woman can't walk on wooden heels, it attracts too much attention! No one gives me anything! No one gives me anything!" And she was so feverish and breathless that no one had the courage to tell her that she would not get them. They only said, "You are not a woman and all shoe heels are made of wood."

Until, just as a person grows fat, she ceased, without knowing through which process, to be precious. There is an obscure law which decrees that the egg be protected until the chicken is born, a bird of fire. And she got her new shoes.

Family Ties

The woman and her mother finally settled back in the taxi that would take them to the station. The mother counted and recounted the two suitcases, trying to convince herself that they were both there. The daughter, with her dark eyes, to which a slight squint gave a constant gleam of derision and indifference, assisted.

"I haven't forgotten anything? her mother asked her for the third time.

"No, no, you haven't forgotten anything," her daughter replied, amused but patient.

She still retained the impression of the almost farcical scene between her mother and her husband at the moment of departure. During the older woman's two-week visit, the two of them had barely endured each other's company; the good-mornings and good-evenings had resounded constantly with a cautious tact which had made her want to smile. But suddenly at the moment of departure, before getting into the taxi, the mother had changed into the exemplary mother-in-law and the husband had become the good son-in-law.

"Please forgive anything I might have said in haste," the older woman had said, and Catherine, with some enjoyment, had seen Tony, unsure of what to do with the suitcases in his hands, stammer—perturbed by his role as the good son-in-law.

"If I laugh they will think I am mad," Catherine had thought, frowning.

"Whoever marries off a son, loses a son, but whoever marries off a daughter gains a son," her mother had added and Tony took advantage of his cold to be able to cough. Standing there, Catherine knowingly observed her husband as his self-assurance disappeared to give place to a slightly built man with a dark complexion, forced into being the son of that grey-haired little woman. . . . It was then that her desire to laugh became stronger. Fortunately she never in fact laughed when she felt the urge: her eyes took on a knowing and restrained expression, they became more squinted, and her laughter showed in her eyes. It always hurt a little to be capable of laughing. But she could do nothing about it: ever since she was a little girl she had laughed through her eyes, and she had always had a squint.

"I still think the child is too thin," her mother said, resisting the bumps of the taxi. And although Tony was not present she was using the same tone of challenge and accusation which she adopted in front of him. So much so that one evening Tony had become exasperated.

"It's not my fault, Severina!" He called his mother-in-law Severina because before the marriage it was decided that they would be a modern mother and son-in-law. Right from her mother's very first visit to the couple, the word Severina had become awkward on her husband's lips, and now, despite the fact that he addressed her by her Christian name, it did not prevent....

Catherine watched them and smiled.

"The child has always been thin, Mother," she replied. The taxi drove on monotonously.

"Thin and highly strung," her mother added decisively.

"Thin and highly strung," assented Catherine patiently.

He was a nervous and distracted child. During his grandmother's visit he had become even more distant and he had started to sleep badly, disturbed by the excessive endearments and affectionate pinching of the older woman. Tony, who had never really given much attention to his son's sensibility, began to make sly digs at his mother-in-law, "for protecting the child...."

"I haven't forgotten anything ..." began her mother again, when a sudden slamming of brakes threw them against each other and sent the suitcases toppling.

"Oh! Oh!" the older woman exclaimed, as if overtaken by some irremediable disaster. "Oh!" she said, swaying her head in surprise, suddenly aged and poor. And Catherine?

Catherine looked at her mother and the mother looked at her daughter. Had some disaster befallen Catherine too? Her eyes blinked with surprise, and she quickly rearranged the suitcases and her handbag in her attempt to remedy the catastrophe as quickly as possible. Because something had, in fact, happened and there was no point in concealing it. Catherine had been thrown against Severina with a physical intimacy long since forgotten, and going back to the days when she belonged to a father and a mother. Although they had never really embraced or kissed each other. With her father, certainly, Catherine had experienced a much closer relationship. When her mother used to fill their plates, forcing them to eat far too much, the two of them used to wink at each other in complicity without her mother even noticing. But after the collision in the taxi and their composure had been restored, they had nothing further to say to each other—both of them feeling anxious to arrive at the station.

"I haven't forgotten anything?" her mother asked with a resigned note.

Catherine neither wanted to meet her eyes again nor make any reply.

"Here are your gloves!" she said, picking them up from the floor.

"Oh! Oh! my gloves!" her mother anxiously exclaimed. They exchanged another glance only when the suitcases had been lifted onto the train and they had exchanged a farewell kiss: her mother's head appeared at the window. It was then that Catherine noticed that her mother had aged and that her eyes were shining.

The train was still waiting to depart and they both lingered without knowing what to say. Her mother took out a mirror from her handbag and studied her new hat, bought from the same milliner patronized by her daughter. She studied herself, putting on an excessively severe expression that betrayed a certain satisfaction with her own appearance. Her daughter observed her with amusement. "No one else can love you except me," thought the woman with a smile in her eyes; and the weight of responsibility put the taste of blood into her mouth. As if "mother and daughter" meant "life and repugnance." No, no, she could not say that she loved her mother. Her mother distressed her, that was it. The old woman had put the mirror back into her handbag and looked at her affectionately. Her face, which was lined but still very expressive, seemed to be forcing itself into making some impression on the other passengers, and here the hat played its part. The station bell suddenly sounded, there was a general movement of alarm, and several people began to run, thinking that the train was already pulling out.

"Mother," said the woman.

"Catherine!" said the old woman. They exchanged frightened glances—a suitcase carried on a porter's head interrupted their view and a youth running past caught Catherine by the arm as he went, disarranging the collar of her dress. When they could see each other again, Catherine was on the point of asking her if she had forgotten anything....

"I haven't forgotten anything?" her mother asked. Catherine, too, had the impression something had been forgotten, and they looked apprehensively at each other—because, if something had really been forgotten, it was too late now. A mother dragged a child along the platform and the child was crying. Once more the station bell sounded....

"Mother," said the woman. What had they forgotten to say to each other? But now it was too late. It seemed to her that the older woman should have said one day, "I am your mother, Catherine," and that she should have replied, "And I am your daughter."

"Don't go sitting in a draught!" Catherine called out.

"Now dear, I am not a child," her mother shouted back, still obviously worrying about her appearance. Her freckled hand, somewhat tremulous, delicately adjusted the brim of her hat and Catherine felt a sudden urge to ask her if she had been happy living with her father.

"Give my love to Auntie!" she shouted.

"Yes, yes."

"Mother," said Catherine, because a prolonged whistle could be heard and the wheels of the train were already moving.

"Catherine!" said the older woman with a gaping mouth and frightened eyes, and with the first jerk the daughter saw her lift her hands to her hat: it had fallen forward covering her nose, so that only her new dentures were showing. The train was already moving and Catherine waved. Her mother's face disappeared for a second and now reappeared, hatless, the topknot on her head undone and falling in white strands over her shoulders like the tresses of a madonna—her head was leaning out and she looked serious, perhaps no longer even able to perceive her daughter in the distance.

Amidst the smoke, Catherine began to walk back down the platform, her eyebrows drawn in a frown and in her eyes the sly look of those with a squint. Relieved of her mother's company, she had recovered her brisk manner of walking; alone it was much easier. Some men were watching her, she was sweet, her body a little on the heavy side perhaps. She walked confidently, looking modern in her outfit, her short hair tinted a reddish brown. And things had disposed themselves in such a way that the sorrow of love seemed to her to be happiness— everything around her was so tender and alive, the dirty street, the old tram cars, orange peel on the pavements—strength flowed to and fro in her heart with a heavy richness. She was very pretty at this moment, so elegant: in harmony with her time and the city where she had been born, almost as if she had chosen it. In her eyes anyone would have perceived the relish this woman had for the things of the world. She studied people with insistence, trying to fix on those inconstant figures a pleasure still moist with tears for her mother. She avoided the cars and managed to approach the bus, circumventing the queue and staring ironically; nothing would prevent this little woman who walked swaying her hips from mounting one more mysterious step in her days.

The elevator droned in the heat of the beach. She opened the door of her apartment with one hand while extricating herself from her little hat with the other; she seemed disposed to take advantage of the largesse of the whole world—a path her mother had opened and that was burning in her breast. Tony scarcely raiséd his eyes from his book. Saturday afternoon had always been "his own" and, immediately after Severina's departure, he returned to it with pleasure, seated at his low desk.

"Has *she* gone?"

"Yes, she's gone," replied Catherine, pushing open the door of her little boy's room. Ah yes, there was her child all right, she thought with sudden relief. Her son. Thin and highly strung. Since the moment he had found his feet, he had started to walk steadily; but, now nearly four years old, he spoke as if verbs were unknown to him: he observed things coldly, unable to connect them among themselves. There he was playing with a wet towel, exact and distant. The woman felt a pleasant warmth and she would have liked to fasten the child forever to this moment; she drew the towel away from him in reproach.

"What a naughty boy!" But the child looked indifferently into the air, communicating with himself. His mind was always somewhere else. No one had yet succeeded in really catching his attention. His mother shook the towel in the air, screening off the view of the room.

"Mummy," said the child. Catherine turned round quickly. It was the first time he had said "Mummy" in that tone without asking for something. It was more than a verification: "Mummy!" The woman continued to shake the towel vigorously and asked herself whom she could tell what had happened, but she did not find anyone who might understand what she herself was at a loss to explain. She stretched the towel out neatly before hanging it up to dry. Perhaps she might be able to tell if she were to change the form. She would relate that her son had said "Mummy, who is God?" No, perhaps "Mummy, child wants God." Perhaps. The truth could only be captured in symbols, and only in symbols would they receive it. With her eyes smiling at her necessary lie and above all at her own foolishness, escaping from Severina, the woman unexpectedly laughed in fact at the child and not only with her eyes; her whole body laughed, broken, her exterior breached and a harshness appearing like a fit of wheezing.

"Ugly," the child then said, examining her.

"Let's go for a walk." she said, coloring and catching him by the hand. She passed through the room, without stopping she advised her husband, "We're going out," and she slammed the apartment door.

Tony had barely time to lift his eyes from his book, and, surprised, he surveyed the room that was already empty.

"Catherine!" he called after her, but the noise of the elevator descending could already be heard. "Where were they going?" he asked himself perturbed, coughing and blowing his nose. Saturdays were "his own," but he liked his wife and child to be at home while he pursued his private occupations. "Catherine!" he called impatiently, although he knew that she could no longer hear him. He got up, went to the window and a moment later spotted his wife and child on the sidewalk.

The two of them had stopped, the woman perhaps deciding which direction to take. And suddenly she was off.

Why was she walking so fast, gripping the child by the hand? From the window he saw his wife holding the child's hand with force and walking quickly, her eyes fixed straight ahead of her; and, even without looking, the man could see the hard expression on her lips. The child—who knows by what dark understanding?—was also staring fixedly ahead, startled and ingenuous. Seen from above, the two figures lost their familiar perspective; they seemed to be flattened to the ground and darker by the light of the sea. The child's hair was blowing in the breeze.

Her husband repeated the question which, even beneath the innocence of a commonplace expression, disturbed him. "Where

are they going? Preoccupied, he watched his wife leading the
child away and he feared that at this moment, when they were
both beyond his reach, she might transmit to their son . . . but
what? "Catherine," he thought, "Catherine, this child is still
innocent!" At what moment was it that a mother, clasping her
child, gave him this prison of love that would descend forever
upon the future man. Later her child, already a man, alone,
would stand before this same window, drumming his fingers
on the windowpane: imprisoned. Obliged to respond to a dead
man. Who would ever know at what moment the mother trans-
ferred her inheritance to her child. And with what morose
pleasure. Now mother and son were understanding each other
within the mystery they shared. Afterward, no one would know
on what black roots man's freedom was nourished. "Catherine,"
he thought, enraged, "the child is innocent!" They had, however, disappeared along the beach. The mystery shared.

"But what about me?" he asked in alarm. The two of them
had gone away on their own. And he had stayed behind. Left
with his Saturday. And his cold. In the tidy apartment, where
"everything worked smoothly." Who knows, perhaps his wife
was escaping with her son from the room, with its carefully
selected pieces of furniture, its curtains and pictures? This is
what he had given her. The apartment of an engineer. And he
knew that if his wife had taken advantage of his situation as a
young husband with a promising future, she also despised the
situation, with those cunning eyes, escaping with her thin,
highly strung child. The man became distressed. Because he
would not be able to give her anything more except—greater
success. Because he knew that she would help him to achieve it
and at the same time would hate what they achieved. Such was
the nature of that serene woman of thirty-two who never really
spoke, as if she had lived since the beginning of time. The relationship between them was so tranquil. At times he tried to

humiliate her by entering the room while she was changing her clothes, because he knew that she detested being seen in the nude. (Why did he find it necessary to humiliate her?)

Meantime, he knew all too well that she would only belong to a man so long as she was proud. But he had got used to making her feminine in this way: he humiliated her with tenderness, and now she was already smiling—without rancor? Perhaps from all this their peaceful relationship had grown, from those quiet conversations that created a family atmosphere for their child. Or this irritated the child at times. At times the child became irritated, he stamped his feet and shouted in his sleep because of some nightmare. From where had that vibrant little fellow emerged, unless from that which his wife and he had cut from their daily life? They lived so tranquilly that, if a moment of happiness approached, they quickly looked at each other, almost ironically, and their eyes said mutually, "Don't let's waste it, don't let's stupidly throw it away"—as if they had lived forever.

But he had watched her from the window, he had seen her walk quickly away, holding the child by the hand, and he had said to himself, "She is taking her moment of happiness—alone." He had felt frustrated because for some time now he could not live with anyone but her. Yet she was able to find her own moments—alone. For instance, what had his wife been up to between the station and the apartment? Not that he suspected her of anything, but his mind was troubled.

The last light of evening fell heavily on the objects in the room. The parched sands cracked. The whole day had languished under the threat of irradiation which did not explode at this moment, although it became more and more deadened and droned in the uninterrupted elevator of the building. When Catherine returned they would dine, warding off the moths. Their child would cry out before falling into a deep sleep and

Catherine would interrupt her dinner for a moment. . . . Wouldn't that elevator halt even for a second? No, the elevator would not halt even for a second.

"After dinner we'll go to the cinema," the man decided. Because after the cinema it would be night at last, and this day would break up like the waves on the rocks of Arpoador.

The Beginnings of a Fortune

It was one of those mornings that seem to be suspended in midair . . . and which come closest to resembling the image we conceive of time.

The veranda was open but the cool air had congealed outside and nothing entered from the garden, as if any influx of air might disturb the harmony. Only some brightly colored flies had penetrated into the dining room and hovered over the sugar bowl. At this hour, Tijuca was still coming to life.

"If only I had some money . . ." thought Arthur, and the desire for treasure . . . to possess peacefully, gave his face a detached and thoughtful expression.

"It's not as if I gamble my money."

"That's enough," his mother replied. "Don't you start that nonsense about money again."

In reality he had no wish to start up any pressing discussion that might end up with a solution. A little of the mortification of last night's dinner when his allowance had been discussed, his father mingling authority with understanding and his mother mingling understanding with basic principles—a little of last night's mortification demanded, meantime, some further discussion. But it was quite useless to pursue, for its own sake, the urgency of the previous day. Each night sleep seemed to respond to all his necessities. And in the morning, in contrast to the adults who got up looking sullen and unshaven, each morning he got up looking younger. His hair was untidy, but not in the same way as his father's disheveled appearance which suggested that something had happened to him during the night. His mother, too, came out of her room looking bedraggled and still drowsy, as if the bitterness of sleep had given her some satisfaction. Until they drank their coffee they were all irritated or pensive, even the maid. This was not the moment to ask for things. But Arthur felt a quiet compulsion to establish his rights in the morning. Each morning he awakened, it was as if he had to recover the previous day—so completely did sleep sever his bonds each night.

"I neither gamble nor waste my money."

"Arthur!" his mother rebuked him sharply, "I have quite enough problems of my own!"

"What problems?" he inquired with sudden interest.

His mother looked at him coldly as if he were a stranger. Yet he was much more of a relation to her than his father, who, in a manner of speaking, had married into the family. She pursed her lips.

"Everybody has their problems, son," she corrected herself, now entering into a new kind of relationship somewhere be-

tween the role of mother and teacher. And from that point on-
ward his mother had taken the day in hand. The suggestion
of individuality with which he had awakened had now disappeared, and Arthur knew that he could count on her. From the
beginning either they always accepted him or reduced him to
being himself. When he was a small child they used to play with
him, they threw him into the air, smothered him with kisses.
Then suddenly they became "individuals"—they put him down
and said kindly but already beyond his reach, "That's enough
now," and he throbbed with their caresses and all those peals
of laughter still in reserve. He would then become cantanker-
ous, and get under their feet, filled with rage which the same
instant would turn to delight, sheer delight, if only they would
relent.

"Eat up, Arthur," concluded his mother, and once more he
knew that he could count on her. So he immediately became
more childish and more difficult.

"I also have my problems but no one takes any notice. When
I say that I need money one would think that I were asking for
money to drink or gamble."

"Since when has it been suggested that it might be for drinking or gambling?" asked his father, coming into the room and
making straight for the head of the table. Whatever next? Such
presumption!

He had not reckoned on his father's arrival. Bewildered, but
accustomed to such moments, he went on.

"But Dad!" his voice became dissonant in a protest that did
not quite amount to indignation. To balance the situation, his
mother was already won over, tranquilly stirring her coffee,
indifferent to the conversation that did not seem to mean anything other than a few more flies to contend with. She waved
them from the sugar bowl with a limp hand.

"It is time you were off," his father interrupted. Arthur turned to his mother. But she was spreading butter on her bread, absorbed and happy. She had escaped again. She would say yes to everything without giving it the slightest importance.

Closing the door, he once again had the impression that they were constantly delivering him to life. That is how the street seemed to receive him. "When I have a wife and children, I'll ring the bell on this side of the door and pay them visits and everything will be different," he thought.

Life outside his home was always completely different. Apart from the difference of light—as if only by going out he could really see what time was doing and what dispositions circumstances had taken during the night—apart from the difference of light there was the difference of his whole manner of existence. When he was little his mother used to say, "Away from home he's an angel and at home a devil."

Even now, going through the little front gate, he had become visibly younger and at the same time less of a child—more sensitive and above all without any matter in hand. But with a docile interest. He was not a person who looked for conversation but if someone asked him as now—"Tell me, son, where is the church?"—he gently came to life, inclined his long neck, because they were always shorter than he, and would guide them, attracted by their question, as if there was an exchange of friendship in this encounter and an open field for investigation. He stood carefully observing the woman turn the corner in the direction of the church, patiently responsible for the route she followed.

"But money is made for spending and you know on what," Charlie insisted vehemently.

"I want it for buying things," he replied somewhat vaguely.

"A little bicycle perhaps?" Charlie smiled offensively, blushing at his own mischief.

Arthur smiled wryly, feeling unhappy.

Seated at his school desk he waited for the teacher to get up.

When the latter cleared his throat as a preface to the beginning of the lesson, it was the usual well-known signal for the pupils to sit back, open their eyes attentively and think about nothing in particular.

"About nothing," was Arthur's troubled reply to the teacher who questioned him with visible annoyance. "About nothing" was vaguely about an earlier conversation, about tentative plans to go to the movies that evening, about—about money. He *needed* money. But during class, when he found himself obliged to sit still and free of any responsibility, every desire had relaxation as its basis.

"Didn't it dawn upon you right away that Glorinha wanted to be invited to go to the movies?" Charlie asked him, and both of them looked inquisitively in the direction of the girl who was walking away, her satchel under her arm. Thoughtfully, Arthur walked on at his chum's side, observing the stones on the ground.

"If you haven't got enough money for two tickets, I'll loan it to you and you can pay me back later."

As far as he could see, the moment he had some money he would be obliged to use it for a thousand and one things.

"But afterward I'll have to pay you back and I already owe money to Tony's brother," he replied evasively.

"So what? Where's the problem?" insisted the other, ever practical and persuasive.

"So what," he thought with subdued rage, "so what, well it looks as if the moment somebody has any money, everyone comes on the scene ready to help you spend it, and to show you how to get rid of it."

"It looks," he said, trying to not to show his anger, "it looks as if you only need a few coppers and some woman gets the scent of it and pounces on you."

The two of them suddenly smiled at each other. After this he felt much more relaxed and confident. Above all, he felt less oppressed by circumstances. But soon it was already midday and any desire became more pressing and difficult to bear. All during lunch he savagely thought whether or not he should get into debt, and he felt himself ruined.

"Either he is studying too hard or he doesn't eat enough at breakfast," his mother complained. The point is that he gets up looking fine but by lunch time he appears with this pale face. Then he starts to look drawn and that's always a bad sign."

"It's nothing serious; naturally he gets tired as the day goes on," replied his father cheerfully. Looking at himself in the mirror in the hall before going out, Arthur recognized that he really had the face of one of those young working lads who always look tired. He smiled without moving his lips, satisfaction showing in the depths of his eyes. But at the theater entrance he had little choice but to ask Charlie for a loan because Glorinha was already there, accompanied by another girl.

"Do you prefer to sit at the front or in the middle?" Glorinha asked.

Confronted with this situation, Charlie paid for the friend and Arthur furtively borrowed the money for Glorinha's ticket.

"Looks as if the outing is ruined," he said in passing to Charlie. Immediately afterward he repented having spoken, since his chum had scarcely heard him, taken up as he was with the other girl. There was no need to lower oneself in the eyes of another chap for whom a session at the movies could only be improved by being with a girl.

In fact, the outing was only ruined at the beginning. Soon afterward his body relaxed, he forgot the presence at his side and became absorbed by the film. Only near the middle was he conscious of Glorinha and with a sudden start watched her secretly. With some surprise, he realized that she was not really the little gold digger he had imagined her to be. Glorinha sat there leaning forward, her mouth attentively open. Relieved, Arthur leaned back again in his seat.

Later, however, he wondered whether he had really been exploited or not. And the anguish was so unbearable that he halted in front of a shop window with an expression of horror. His heart was thumping like a piston. In addition to his frightened face, disembodied in the glass of the window, there were saucepans and kitchen utensils that he looked at with a certain familiarity.

"It looks as if I have been exploited," he resolved, and yet he could not superimpose his anger on Glorinha's innocent profile. Gradually the girl's innocence itself became her major crime: so she was exploiting him, she had exploited him and then sat there thoroughly satisfied with herself watching the film? And his eyes filled with tears. "The ungrateful wretch," he thought, awkwardly choosing a word of accusation. As the word was a symbol of complaint rather than anger, he became a little confused and his anger abated. It now seemed to him, looking at it objectively and freely, that she should have been forced to pay for the movie.

But, confronted by his books and notes closed before him, his face brightened.

He no longer heard the doors that banged, the piano of the woman next door, his mother's voice on the telephone. There was a great silence in the room as if in a vault. And the late afternoon gave the impression of morning. He felt remote . . . so remote, like a giant on the outside with only his absorbed fingers, which kept on turning a pencil backward and forward, penetrating the room. There were moments when he breathed heavily like an old man. The greater part of the time, however, his face barely came to the surface of the air in the room.

"I've already finished my homework!" he called to his mother, who had questioned the noise of running water. Carefully washing his feet in the bath, he reflected that Glorinha's friend was preferable to Glorinha herself. Nor had he made any attempt to observe if Charlie had or had not "taken advantage" of the other girl. At this idea, he quickly stepped out of the bath and paused in front of the mirror above the wash basin—until the tiled floor chilled his wet feet.

No! He had nothing to explain to Charlie and no one would tell him how to spend whatever money he had, and Charlie could believe that he spent it on bicycles. And if he did—what was wrong with that? And if he should never, but never wish to spend his money? And suppose he were to get richer and richer? What's wrong with that? Are you looking for a fight? You think that. . . .

"You may be lost in your thoughts," his mother said, interrupting him, "but at least eat your dinner and try to make some conversation."

Then, suddenly restored to the family circle, he protested. "You always say that one shouldn't talk at the table, and now you want me to talk; you told me not to speak with my mouth full, now. . . ."

"Mind your manners when you are addressing your mother," his father said without severity.

"Dad," Arthur replied meekly, with furrowed eyebrows, "Dad, what is a promissory note?"

"It looks as if high school is not doing you much good," his father said with quiet satisfaction.

"Eat more potatoes, Arthur," persuaded his mother, vainly trying to draw the two men to herself.

"A promissory note," explained his father, pushing away his plate, "is the following: let us suppose that you are in debt. . . ."

Mystery in São Cristóvão

On an autumn evening, with tall, erect hyacinths beside the windowpane, the dining room of a house was lit up and peaceful.

Around the table, motionless for a moment, the father, mother, grandmother, three children, and a slender nineteen-year-old girl. The cool perfumed night air of São Cristóvão was in no sense dangerous, but the way in which the members of the household were grouped inside the house precluded everything except an intimate family circle on such a cool May evening.

There was nothing special about the gathering: they had just had dinner and they sat talking round the table, while mosquitoes circled the light. What made the scene so particularly complete and the expression of everyone there so relaxed, was the fact that after many years one could almost feel, at long last, the progress of this family. Now, on this autumn evening, after dinner, here are the children who diligently attend school each day, the father who devotes himself to his business, the mother who for many years has been bearing children and doing the housework, the young girl who has been adapting herself to a delicate phase of maturity, and the grandmother who has reached her old age. Without realizing it, the family gazed upon that room with deep satisfaction, watching the rare moment of May and its abundance.

Then each retired to his room. The old woman stretched herself out, sighing with benevolence. The father and mother, after locking up the house, lay down pensively and fell asleep. The three children, choosing the most awkward positions, slept in three beds, as on three trapezes. The young girl in her cotton nightgown opened her window and inhaled the whole garden, restless yet happy. Disturbed by the fragrant humidity, she lay down, promising herself a completely new outlook tomorrow which would shake the hyacinths and make the fruits tremble on the branches—and in the midst of her meditation she fell asleep.

The hours passed. And when the silence twinkled in the glow of fireflies—the children suspended in their sleep, the grand-mother, pondering over a difficult dream, the parents fatigued, the young girl asleep in the midst of her meditation—the doors of a house on the corner opened and three masqueraders stepped out.

The first was tall and wore the head mask of a rooster. The second was fat and was dressed up as a bull. And the third, who was younger, for want of a better idea, had disguised himself as an ancient knight and wore a demon's mask, through which appeared two innocent eyes. The three masqueraders crossed the road in silence.

When they passed the house of our family, which was now in darkness, the man masquerading as a rooster (who invented nearly all the ideas for that trio) suddenly stopped and nudged his companions.

"Just take a look."

His companions, reduced to patience by the utter discomfort of their masks, obeyed him and saw a house with a garden. Feeling elegant, but miserable, they waited patiently for their leader to continue with what he had to say. Finally the rooster said, "We can gather hyacinths."

The other two made no reply. They took advantage of their halt in order to examine, in discomfort, their appearance and to find some way of breathing more freely inside those masks.

"A hyacinth for each of us to pin on to his costume," the rooster concluded.

The bull fidgeted nervously at the idea of yet another decoration to keep an eye on during the festivities. But, after a moment in which the three of them seemed to be deeply absorbed in reaching a decision, without, in fact, deciding anything, the rooster strode ahead, gingerly climbed over the railings, and stepped onto the forbidden territory of the garden. The bull followed him with some difficulty. But the knight, although hesitant, with one mighty leap landed right among the hyacinths with a dull thud that riveted all three of them to the spot in terror. Too frightened to breathe, the rooster, the bull, and the demon knight scrutinized the darkness. But the house remained among shadows and toads. And in the garden, suffused with perfume, the hyacinths trembled unconcerned.

Then the rooster advanced. He could pick the hyacinth that was within his reach. The larger flowers, however, which grew beside a window—tall, brittle, fragile—stood glittering and beckoned to him. On tiptoe the rooster made his way toward them, the bull and the knight following behind. The silence kept watch over them.

But just as he was on the point of breaking the stalk of the largest hyacinth, the rooster froze in his tracks. The other two halted with a sigh that plunged them into sleep.

Behind the dark glass of the window a white face was watching them.

The rooster had frozen in the gesture of plucking the hyacinth. The bull remained with his hands still uplifted. The knight, ashen under his mask, became a little boy again confronting the fears of his childhood. The face behind the window steadily watched them.

None of the four would ever know which was the punishment of the other. The hyacinths gradually seemed to become whiter in the darkness.

Paralyzed, the masqueraders stood peering at each other. The simple encounter of four masks on that autumn evening seemed to have touched deep recesses, then others, and still others which, had it not been for the moment in the garden, would have remained forever with this perfume which is in the air and in the immanence of those four natures which fate had designated, assigning the hour and place—the same precise fate of a falling star. These four, having come from reality, had become subject to the possibilities an autumn evening possesses in São Cristóvão. Each humid plant, each pebble, the hoarse toads—all of them exploiting the silent chaos in order to arrange themselves in a better spot—everything in that darkness silently approached. Having fallen into the ambush, they looked at each other in fear: the nature of things had been surpassed and the four figures spied each other with open wings. The rooster, the bull, the demon, and the girl's face had unraveled the marvels of the garden. That was when the great May moon appeared.

It was a dangerous moment for the four images. So fraught with danger that, without a murmur, the four mute apparitions retreated without taking their eyes off each other, fearing that the moment they no longer held each other in their gaze, new remote territories would be ravaged, and that after their silent defeat the hyacinths would remain in possession of the garden's treasure. No specter saw the other disappear because they all withdrew at the same time, slowly, on tiptoe. No sooner, however, had the magic circle of the four been broken, liberated from their mutual vigilance, than the stars dissolved in terror. Three figures sprang like cats over the garden railings, and another, petrified and enlarged, drew away backward as far as the threshold of a doorway, where, screaming, it started to run.

The three masked gentlemen who, at the rooster's fatal suggestion, aimed to cause some surprise at a ball in a season so remote from Carnival, caused a sensation in the midst of the festivities that were already under way. The band stopped playing and the dancers, still holding their partners, saw, among peals of laughter, three breathless masqueraders fumble like beggars in the entrance. Finally, after several attempts, the guests had to abandon the idea of making them the main attraction of the evening, because in their terror the masqueraders refused to let go of one another: the tall one, the fat one, the young one, the fat one, the young one, the tall one, contrast and unity, their speechless faces beneath three masks which faltered independently.

Meanwhile, the house of the hyacinths was now all lit up. The young girl was sitting in the hall. The grandmother, with her white hair in braids, held a glass of water, her hand smoothing the girl's dark hair while the father chased through the house. The young girl was unable to explain: she appeared to have said everything with her scream. Her face grew small and bright—the whole laborious structure of her years had dissolved and she was a child once more. But in her rejuvenated image, to the horror of the family, a white strand had appeared among the hairs on her forehead. Since she persisted in staring in the direction of the window, they left her to rest and, armed with candlesticks and shivering with cold in their nightgowns, they went out to explore the garden.

Soon the candles scattered, dancing in the darkness. The ivy plants exposed to light immediately curled up, the toads illuminated, jumped among their feet, fruits were golden for a second among the leaves. The garden, aroused from a dream, now seemed to expand, now to fade away; butterflies hovered like sleepwalkers. Finally, the old lady, long familiar with the flowerbeds, pointed to the only visible sign in the garden that shunned discovery: the hyacinth—still alive but with its stalk broken. . . . Then it was true: something had happened. They returned indoors, put on all the lights in the house, and spent the rest of the night—waiting.

Only the three children continued to sleep ever more soundly; the young girl gradually recovered her true years. She alone did not continue to look for something. But the others, who had seen nothing, became watchful and unsettled. And since the progress in that family was the fragile product of many solicitudes and some deceptions, everything dissolved and had to be restored almost from the beginning: the grandmother once again quick to take offense, the father and mother fatigued, the children intolerable, the whole house appearing to lie in wait for that breeze of plenitude to blow once more after dinner. Perhaps it would happen some other autumn evening.

The Crime of the Mathematics Professor

When the man reached the highest hill, the bells were ringing in the city below. The uneven rooftops of the houses could barely be seen. Near him was the only tree on the plain. The man was standing with a heavy sack in his hand.

His near-sighted eyes looked down below. Catholics, crawling and minute, were going into church, and he tried to hear the scattered voices of the children playing in the square. But despite the clearness of the morning hardly a sound reached the plateau. He also saw the river which seen from above seemed motionless, and he thought: it is Sunday. In the distance he saw the highest mountain with its dry slopes. It was not cold but he pulled his overcoat tighter for greater protection. Finally he placed the sack carefully on the ground. He took off his spectacles, perhaps in order to breathe more easily, because he found that clutching his spectacles in his hand he could breathe more deeply. The light beat on the lenses, which sent out sharp signals. Without his spectacles, his eyes blinked brightly, appearing almost youthful and unfamiliar. He replaced his spectacles and became once more a middle-aged man and grabbed hold of the sack again: it was as heavy as if it were made of stone, he thought. He strained his sight in order to see the current of the river, and tilted his head trying to hear some sound: the river seemed motionless and only the harshest sound of a voice momentarily reached that height—yes, he felt fine up here. The cool air was inhospitable for one who had lived in a warm city. The only tree on the plain swayed its branches. He watched it. He was gaining time. Until he felt that there was no need to wait any longer.

And meantime he kept watch. His spectacles certainly bothered him because he removed them again, sighed deeply, and put them in his pocket.

He opened his sack and peered inside. Then he put his scrawny hand inside and slowly drew out the dead dog. His whole being was concentrated on that vital hand and he kept his eyes tightly shut as he pulled. When he opened them, the air was clearer still and the happy bells rang out again, summoning the faithful to the solace of punishment.

The unknown dog lay exposed.

He now set to work methodically. He grabbed the rigid black dog and laid it on a shallow piece of ground. But, as if he had already achieved a great deal, he put on his spectacles, sat down beside the dog's carcass, and began to contemplate the landscape.

He saw quite clearly, and with a certain sense of futility, the deserted plain. But he accurately observed that when seated he could no longer see the minute city below. He sighed again. Rummaging in his sack, he drew out a spade and started thinking about the spot he would choose. Perhaps below the tree. He surprised himself, reflecting that he would bury this dog beneath the tree. But if it were the other, the real dog, he would bury it in fact where he himself would like to be buried were he dead: in the very center of the plateau, facing the sun with empty eyes. Then, since the unknown dog was, in fact, a substitute for the "other one," he decided that the former, for the greater perfection of the act, should receive exactly the same treatment as the latter would have received. There was no confusion in the man's mind. He understood himself with cold deliberation and without any loose threads.

Soon, in an excess of scruples, he was absorbed in trying to determine accurately the center of the plateau. It was not easy because the only tree rose on one side, and by accepting it as a false center, it divided the plain asymmetrically. Confronted with this difficulty, the man admitted, "It was unnecessary to bury in the center. I should also bury the other, let us say, right here, where I am standing at this very moment." It was a question of bestowing on the event the inevitability of chance, the mark of an external and evident occurrence—on the same plane as the children in the square and the Catholics entering church —it was a question of making the fact as visible as possible on the surface of the world beneath the sky. It was a question of exposing oneself and of exposing a fact, and of not permitting that fact the intimate and unpunished form of a thought.

The idea of burying the dog where he was standing at that very moment caused the man to draw back with an agility which his small and singularly heavy body did not permit. Because it seemed to him that under his feet the outline of the dog's grave had been drawn.

Then he started to dig rhythmically with his spade at that very spot. At times he interrupted his work to take off and put back on his spectacles. He was sweating profusely. He did not dig deeply, but not because he wished to spare himself fatigue. He did not dig deeply because he clearly thought, "If the grave were for the real dog, I should only dig a shallow hole and I would bury it quite close to the surface." He felt that the dog on the surface of the earth would not lose its sensibility.

Finally he put his spade aside, gently lifted the unknown dog and placed it in the grave. What a strange face that dog had. When, with a shock, he had discovered the dead dog on a street corner, the idea of burying it had made his heart so heavy and surprised that he had not even had eyes for that hard snout and congealed saliva. It was a strange, objective dog.

The dog was a little bigger than the hole he had excavated, and after being covered with earth it would be a barely perceptible mound of earth on the plain. This was exactly as he wanted it. He covered the dog with earth and flattened the ground with his hands, feeling its form in his palms with care and pleasure, as if he were smoothing it again and again. The dog was now merely a part of the land's appearance.

Then the man got up, shook the earth from his hands and did not look back even once at the grave. He reflected with a certain satisfaction, "I think I have done everything." He gave a deep sigh, and an innocent smile of release. Yes, he had done everything. His crime had been punished and he was free.

And now he could think freely about the real dog, something he had avoided so far. The real dog which at that very moment must be wandering bewildered through the streets of the other county, sniffing out that city where he no longer had a master.

He then began to think with difficulty about the real dog as if he were trying to think with difficulty about his real life. The fact that the dog was far away in another city made his task difficult, although his yearning drew him close to the memory.

"While I made you in my image, you made me in yours," he thought, then, aided by his yearning, "I called you Joe in order to give you a name that might serve you as a soul at the same time. And you? How shall I ever know the name you gave me? How much more you loved me than I loved you," he reflected with curiosity.

"We understood each other too well, you with the human name I gave you, I with the name you gave me, and which you never pronounced except with your insistent gaze," the man thought, smiling with affection, now free to remember at will.

"I recall when you were little," he thought in amusement, "so small, cute, and frail, wagging your tail, watching me, and my discovering in you a new form of possessing my soul. But from that moment, you were already becoming each day a dog whom one could abandon. In the meantime our pranks became dangerous with so much understanding," the man recalled with satisfaction, "you finished up biting me and snarling; I ended up throwing a book at you and laughing. But who knows what that reluctant smile of mine already meant. Each day you became a dog whom one could abandon."

"And how you sniffed the streets!" the man thought, laughing a little, "indeed you did not pass a single stone without sniffing . . . that was the childish side to your nature. Or was that your true destiny in being a dog? And the rest merely a joke in being mine? For you were tenacious. And, calmly wagging your tail, you seemed to refuse in silence the name I had given you. Ah yes, you were tenacious. I did not want you to eat meat so that you would not become ferocious, but one day you jumped up on the table and, among the happy shouts of the children, you grabbed the meat, and with a ferocity that does not come from eating, you watched me, silent and tenacious, with the meat in your mouth. Because, although mine, you never conceded me even a little of your past or your nature. And, troubled, I began to realize that you did not ask of me that I should yield anything of mine in order to love you, and this began to annoy me. It was on this point of the resistant reality of our two natures that you hoped we might understand each other. My ferocity and yours must not exchange themselves for sweetness; it was this which you were teaching me little by little, and it was this, too, which was becoming unbearable. In asking nothing of me, you were asking too much. Of yourself, you demanded that you should be a dog. Of me, you demanded that I should be a man. And I, I pretended as much as I could. At times, crouched on your paws before me, how you watched me! I would then look at the ceiling, I would cough, look away, examine my fingernails. But nothing moved you, and you went on watching me. Whom were you going to tell? 'Pretend,' I said to myself, 'pretend quickly that you are another, arrange a false meeting, caress him, throw him a bone,' but nothing distracted you as you watched me. What an idiot I was. I trembled with horror, when you were the innocent one: that I should turn round and suddenly show you my real face, and that I should trap you, your hairs bristling, and carry you to the door wounded forever. Oh, each day you became a dog that could be abandoned. One could choose. But you, trustfully, wagged your tail.

"Sometimes, impressed by your alertness, I succeeded in seeing in you your own anguish. Not the anguish of being a dog, which was your only possible form. But the anguish of existing in such a perfect way that it became an unbearable happiness: you would then leap and come to lick my face with a love entirely given, and a certain danger of hatred as if it were I who had revealed you to yourself through friendship. Now I am quite certain that it was not I who possessed a dog. It was you who possessed a person.

"But you possessed a person so powerful that he could choose: and then he abandoned you. With relief he abandoned you. With relief, yes, because you demanded—with the serene and simple incomprehension of a truly heroic dog—that I should be a man. He abandoned you with an excuse supported by everyone at home. How could I move house and baggage and children—and on top of that a dog—with the business of adapting to the new school and a new city, and on top of that a dog? 'There is no room for him anywhere,' said Martha, as practical as ever. 'He will disturb the other passengers,' my mother-in-law added, not knowing that I had already justified my decision, and the children cried, and I did not look either at them or you, Joe. But only you and I know that I abandoned you because you were the constant possibility of the crime I never committed. The possibility of my sinning which, in the pretense of my eyes, was already a sin. I then sinned at once in order to be blamed at once. And this crime replaces the greater crime which I should not have had the courage to commit," thought the man, becoming ever more lucid.

"There are so many forms of being guilty and of losing oneself forever, and to betray oneself and not to confront oneself. I chose that of wounding a dog," the man thought. "Because I knew that this would be a minor offense and that no one goes to hell for abandoning a dog that trusted in a human. For I knew that this crime was not punishable."

Seated on the mountain top, his mathematical head was cold and intelligent. Only now did he seem to understand, in his icy awareness, that he had done something with the dog that was truly irrevocable and beyond punishment. They still had not invented a punishment for the great concealed crimes and for the deep betrayals.

A man still succeeded in being more astute than the Last Judgment. This crime was condemned by no one. Not even the Church. They are all my accomplices, Joe. I should have to knock from door to door and beg them to accuse and punish me: they would all slam the door on me with a sudden look of hostility. No one will condemn this crime of mine. Not even you, Joe, will condemn me. Powerful as I am, I need only choose to call you. Abandoned in the streets, you would come leaping to lick my face with contentment and forgiveness. I would give you my other face to kiss.

The man took off his spectacles, sighed, and put them on again. He looked at the covered grave where he had buried an unknown dog in tribute to his abandoned dog, trying, after all, to pay the debt which, disturbingly, no one was claiming—trying to punish himself with an act of kindness and to rid himself of his crime. Like someone giving alms in order to be able to eat at last the cake which deprived the beggar of bread.

But as if Joe, the dog he had abandoned, were demanding of him much more than a lie; as if he were demanding that he, in one last effort, might prove himself a man—and as such assume the responsibility of his crime—he looked at the grave where he had buried his weakness and his condition.

And now, even more mathematical, he sought a way to eliminate that self-inflicted punishment. He must not be consoled. He coldly searched for a way of destroying the false burial of the unknown dog. He then bent down, and, solemn and calm, he unburied the dog with a few simple movements. The dark form of the dog at last appeared whole and unfamiliar with earth on its eyelashes, its eyes open and crystallized. And so the mathematics professor had renewed his crime forever. The man then looked around him and up to the skies, pleading for a witness to what he had done. And, as if that were still not enough, he began to descend the slopes, heading toward the intimacy of his home.

The Buffalo

But it was spring. Even the lion licked the smooth head of the lioness. Two golden animals. The woman looked away from the cage, where only the warm scent reminded her of the carnage she had come in search of in the zoological gardens. Then the lion passed, heavy-maned and tranquil, and the lioness, her head on her outstretched paws, slowly became a sphinx once more.

"But this is love, this is love again," the woman said in rebellion, trying to find her own hatred, but it was spring and the two lions were in love. With her hands in her coat pockets, she looked around to find herself surrounded by cages, and caged by locked cages. She walked on. Her eyes were so intent upon her search that at times her sight darkened in slumber, and then she felt refreshed as in the coolness of a cave.

But the giraffe was a virgin with newly shorn braids. With the simple-minded innocence of that which is large and light and without guilt. The woman in the brown coat looked away —sick, so sick. Unable—confronted with that lovely giraffe standing before her, that silent wingless bird—unable to find within herself the critical point of her illness, the sickest point, the point of hatred, she who had gone to the zoological gardens in order to be sick. But not in the presence of the giraffe, which was more landscape than being. Not in the presence of that flesh which had strayed in height and distance, that giraffe which was almost green. She sought out other animals and tried to learn from them how to hate. The hippopotamus, the humid hippopotamus. Its round mass of flesh, its round, mute flesh awaiting some other round, mute flesh. No. Then there was such a humble love in maintaining oneself only as flesh, there was such a sweet martyrdom in not knowing how to think.

But it was spring, and, clenching her fists in her coat pockets, she would have destroyed those monkeys leaping around inside the cages, monkeys as happy as larks, monkeys tamely leaping among themselves, one female monkey with the resigned look of love and another engaged in breast-feeding. She would have destroyed them with fifteen sharp bullets: the woman's teeth clenched until her jawbone hurt. The nakedness of those monkeys. That world which saw no danger in being nude. She would have destroyed their nudity. An ape, too, looked at her holding on to the bars, its scrawny arms opened in the form of a crucifix, its hairy chest exposed without pride. But she would not aim for its chest, it was between the ape's eyes that she would aim, between those eyes which stared at her unblinking. Suddenly the woman averted her gaze: the ape's eyes had a white gelatinous veil covering the pupils and in their expression the sweetness of illness. It was an old ape—the woman turned her eyes away, clenching between her teeth a sentiment she had not come in search of: she hastened her steps, still looking back in terror at the ape with outspread arms. He continued to stare ahead of him.

"Oh no, not this," she thought and as she escaped, she pleaded, "God, teach me only to hate."

"I hate you," she said to a man whose only crime was not to love her. "I hate you," she gasped in haste. But she did not even know how to begin. How to dig in the earth until she would find the black water, how to open a passage in the hard soil and never find herself? She walked through the zoological gardens among mothers and their children. But the elephant supported its own weight. That whole elephant which had the power to crush at will simply with its foot. Yet which failed to crush anything. That power which meantime would meekly allow itself to be led to a circus, an elephant for children. And its eyes were as kind as those of an old man, fixed within its great inherited flesh. The oriental elephant. An oriental springtime too, and everything coming to life, everything running through the stream.

The woman then tried the camel. The ragged humpbacked camel chewing on itself, absorbed in the process of recognizing its food. She felt weak and fatigued and for two days she had scarcely eaten. The camel's long dusty eyelashes shielded eyes that had dedicated themselves to the patience of its internal craft. Patience, patience, patience—this alone did she encounter in the spring breeze. Tears filled the woman's eyes, tears that did not flow, arrested within the patience of her inherited flesh. Only the camel's dusty odor came in opposition to what she had come for—dry hatred, not tears. She approached the bars of the enclosure, she inhaled the dust of that old carpet where ashen blood circulated. She sought the impure warmth, and pleasure pervaded her shoulders to the point of uneasiness, but it was not yet that uneasiness which she craved. In her stomach the urge to destroy contracted itself in colic. But not the tow-colored camel.

"Oh God, who will be my partner in this world?"

Then she was alone in possessing her violence. In the small amusements park of the zoological gardens she waited pensively in the queue of lovers for her turn to take a seat in the car of the roller coaster.

And now she was in her seat, silent in her brown coat. The car still stationary, the machinery of the roller coaster still at a halt. Alone in her seat she seemed to be sitting in a church. Lowering her eyes she saw the ground between the tracks. The ground where simply for love—love, love, not love—where for pure love there sprang up among the tracks weeds of a green so soft and ridiculous that they forced her to avert her gaze, tortured by temptation. The breeze made the hair on the nape of her neck stand on end; she trembled, refusing, refusing the temptation—it was always so much easier—to love.

But suddenly there was that soaring of entrails, that arrested heartbeat taken unaware in midair, the terror, the triumphant fury with which the car precipitated her into emptiness and suddenly raised her like a doll with lifted skirts, the deep resentment with which she became mechanical, her body automatically buoyant—the shrieks of girls with their boyfriends! —her gaze pierced by her utter surprise, her humiliation, "they were doing what they liked with her," the terrible humiliation —the shrieks of girls with their boyfriends!—the utter bewilderment of this spasmodic game as they did what they liked with her and her innocence was suddenly exposed. How many seconds? The seconds necessary for the prolonged whistle of a train taking a bend, and the joy of a new dive through the air insulting her with a kick from behind, as she danced out of step in the wind, danced frenziedly, whether she liked it or not, her body convulsed like that of someone laughing, the sensation of death in a fit of laughter, the death without warning of someone who did not have time to destroy the papers in his drawers beforehand, not the death of others, but her death, always hers. She, who could have taken advantage of the cries of the others to utter her howl of agony, forgot herself, and she only felt fear.

And now this silence which was also sudden. They were back on the ground, the machinery once more completely at a standstill. Pallid, thrown out of her church, she looked at the motionless ground which she had left behind and to which once more she had been delivered. She straightened her skirt cautiously without looking at anyone. Contrite, as on the day when in full view of a crowd everything had spilled from her handbag to the ground and everything which had retained some value while secret in her bag, once exposed in the dust of the road, had revealed the pettiness of an intimate life marked by precautions: face powder, a receipt, her fountain pen—gathering the props of her existence from the curbstone. She got out of the car feeling stunned as if she were shaking off a collision. Although no one appeared to notice her, she smoothed her skirt again, doing her utmost that the others should not observe that she felt weak and sullied, protecting her disrupted bones with pride. The sky went round and round in her empty stomach; the earth, moving up and down before her eyes, seemed remote at certain moments, the earth which is always so obscure. For an instant, the woman desired, in the exhaustion of silent weeping, to reach out with her hand to the obscure earth: her hand stretched itself out like that of a cripple begging alms. But, as if she had swallowed emptiness, her heart was taken by surprise. Only this? Only this? Of her violence, only this?

She started to move once more in the direction of the animals. The tumult of the roller coaster had left her subdued. She felt unable to walk much further and rested her head on the bars of a cage, exhausted, her breath becoming short and faint. From inside its cage, the coati watched her. She looked at him. No words were exchanged. She would never be able to hate that coati, which in the silence of its questioning form watched her. Perturbed, she turned her eyes away from the ingenuous coati. The inquisitive coati asked her a question like a child. While she looked away, concealing her mortal mission from him, her head was resting so close to the bars that for a second it seemed to her that she was the one who was caged while a liberated coati was examining her.

The cage was always on the side where she was: she gave a groan that seemed to come from the soles of her feet. Then yet another groan.

Rising from her womb, there came once more, imploring and in a slow wave, the urge to destroy. Her eyes moistened, grateful and black, in something near to happiness. It was not yet hatred; as yet it was only the tortured will to hate possessing her like some desire, the promise of a cruel flowering, a torment as of love, the craving for hatred promising itself sacred blood and triumph, and the spurned female had spiritualized herself in great expectancy. But where, where would she find the animal that might teach her to keep her own hatred? That hatred which belonged to her by right but which she could not attain in grief? Where would she learn to hate so as not to die of love? And with whom? The world of spring, the world of beasts that in the spring grew spiritual, with paws which scratch but do not wound. . . . Ah! no more of this world! No more of this perfume, nor this weary heaving, no more of this pardoning everything that will die one day as if it were in the act of surrendering. Pardon never—if that woman should ever pardon again, even if it were only once more, her life would be lost—she gave a harsh, broken sob that startled the coati. Caged, she looked around her, and as she was not the sort of person others might notice, she crouched like a solitary old murderess as a child ran past without seeing her.

She started walking again, now shrunken, brittle, her

clenched hands once more mortified in her pockets, the unknown murderess. Everything was imprisoned in her breast—in that breast which only knew how to accept, to resign itself, which only knew how to ask pardon, knew how to pardon, which had only learned to possess the sweetness of unhappiness, and how to love, to love, to love. To imagine that perhaps she had never experienced the hatred of which her pardon had always been made, caused her heart to grieve without shame, and she began to walk so quickly that she appeared to have found a sudden destiny. Almost running, her shoes unbalanced her and gave her body an appearance of fragility that once more reduced her to a female in captivity. Her steps mechanically assumed the imploring desperation of the fragile, she who was nothing more than fragile. But if she could throw off her shoes, would she be able to avoid the happiness of going barefooted? How could one fail to love the ground one treads? Sobbing once more, she stopped in front of the bars of an enclosure and rested her feverish brow against the rusty coldness of the iron. Her eyes firmly closed, she tried to bury her face between the hardness of the bars, and her face searched for an impossible entrance between the narrow bars, just as she had previously seen the newborn monkey search in the blindness of its hunger for its mother's breast. A fleeting comfort came to her from the way in which the bars seemed to hate her, opposing her with the resistance of cold iron.

She slowly opened her eyes. Those eyes emerging from their own darkness saw nothing in the faint light of evening. She stood there breathing. Little by little she began once more to perceive, little by little, forms began to solidify, her weary body overpowered by the sweetness of her fatigue. Her searching gaze turned toward the trees with their sprouting buds and her eyes met the small white clouds. Without hope, she heard the gentle current of a brook. Lowering her head once more, she stood watching the buffalo in the distance. Dressed in a brown coat, breathing without interest, no one interested in her, she herself interested in no one.

A certain peace at last. The breeze was playing with the hair on her head like that of someone who had just died, their head still perspiring. She contemplated with detachment that wide dry expanse enclosed by high railings, the territory of the buffalo. The black buffalo stood still at the bottom of the enclosure. Then he sauntered with his narrow haunches, his compact haunches. His neck was thicker than his contracted flanks. Seen from the front, the buffalo's head, which was much larger than his body, like a severed head, prevented any view of the rest of his body. And on his head his horns. In the distance his great torso paraded slowly. He was a black buffalo. So black that from a distance his face had no features. Over the blackness rose the elevated whiteness of his horns.

The woman might have gone away but the silence soothed her as evening fell.

And in the silence of the enclosure, the slow steps of the buffalo, the dry dust under his dry hoofs. From afar, pacing tranquilly, the black buffalo looked at her for a moment. The next moment, the woman could barely distinguish the hard muscle of its body. Perhaps he had not seen her. She could not tell, because from the shadows of its head she could only distinguish the outlines. But once more he seemed to have seen her or felt her presence.

The woman straightened her head a little and retreated slightly in distrust. Keeping quite still, her head drawn back, she waited.

And once again the buffalo appeared to observe her. As if unable to bear what she had felt, she averted her gaze and contemplated a tree. Her heart no longer beat in her breast, but felt hollow in the pit of her stomach.

The buffalo broke into another slow canter. The dust rose.

The woman clenched her teeth, her whole face smarting slightly.

The buffalo with its black back. In the luminous light of the approaching evening, his was a blackened shape of tranquil fury. The woman sighed softly. Something white had spread itself inside her, white as paper, fragile as paper, intense as whiteness. Death hummed in her ears. Another canter by the buffalo brought her back to her senses, and in another long sigh she came back to the surface. She did not know where she had been. She was on her feet and feeling extremely weak, having emerged from that white remote thing where she had been— from where she now looked at the buffalo. The buffalo now appeared to be larger. The black buffalo once more.

"Ah!" she exclaimed suddenly in pain. The buffalo with its back to her, motionless. The woman's pallid face did not know how to summon him.

"Ah!" she exclaimed, provoking him. Her face was transformed by a deathly pallor and with a sudden, emaciated look, assumed an expression of purity and veneration.

"Ah!" she incited him with clenched teeth. But with his back to her, the buffalo remained quite still. She picked up a pebble from the ground and threw it inside the enclosure. The immobility of the buffalo's torso, which seemed even blacker than before, remained impassive. The pebble rolled away—quite useless.

"Ah!" she cried, shaking the bars. That white thing spread itself inside her, viscous like saliva. The buffalo remained with his back to her.

"Ah!" she cried. But this time there flowed inside her at last the first trickle of black blood. The initial moment was one of pain. As if the world had shriveled up so that this blood might flow. She stood there, hearing that first bitter oil drip as in a grotto, the shunned female. Her strength was still imprisoned between the bars, but something incomprehensible and warm, something incomprehensible, was happening, something that tasted in the mouth like happiness. Then the buffalo turned around.

The buffalo turned around, stood rigid, and, from afar, looked at her.

"I love you," she said, out of hatred then for the man whose great and unpunishable crime was not loving her, "I hate you," she said, imploring love from the buffalo.

Provoked at last, the great buffalo approached without haste.

He approached and the dust rose. The woman waited, her arms drooping down alongside her coat. Slowly he approached. She did not retreat a single step until he reached the bars and halted. There stood the buffalo and the woman face to face. She looked neither at his face, nor his mouth, nor his horns. She looked at his eyes.

And the eyes of the buffalo—his eyes met her eyes. And a pallor so deep was exchanged that, drowsily, the woman grew numb. She was on her feet but in a trance. Small, crimson eyes watched her. The eyes of the buffalo. The woman staggered in amazement and slowly shook her head. The buffalo remained calm. The woman slowly shook her head, terrified by the hatred with which the buffalo, tranquil with hatred, watched her. Almost feigning innocence, she stood shaking her head in disbelief, her mouth ajar. Innocent, inquisitive, entering ever more into those eyes that fixed her without haste, ingenuous, wearily sighing, without wishing nor being able to escape, she was caught in mutual assassination. Caught as if her hand had fastened forever to the dagger that she herself had thrust. Caught, as she slipped spellbound along the railings—overcome by such giddiness that, before her body toppled gently to the ground, the woman saw the entire sky and a buffalo.

CPSIA information can be obtained
at www.ICGtesting.com
Printed in the USA
FSHW010358080120
65783FS